Cutie Pie Must Die

A Troy Murdock
and Zane Ward Mystery

Visit us at www.boldstrokesbooks.com

CUTIE PIE MUST DIE

A TROY MURDOCK
AND ZANE WARD MYSTERY

by

R. W. Clinger

A Division of Bold Strokes Books

2013

CUTIE PIE MUST DIE

ISBN 13: 978-1-60282-961-9

THIS TRADE PAPERBACK ORIGINAL IS PUBLISHED BY
BOLD STROKES BOOKS, INC.
P.O. BOX 249
VALLEY FALLS, NY 12185

FIRST EDITION: NOVEMBER 2013

CREDITS
EDITORS: GREG HERREN AND STACIA SEAMAN
PRODUCTION DESIGN: STACIA SEAMAN
COVER DESIGN BY SHERI (GRAPHICARTIST2020@HOTMAIL.COM)

Acknowledgments

A mystery is never written alone. I would like to thank the following readers for all of their help in creating *Cutie Pie Must Die*:

Alexandro Padilla
Faye Worthington
Greg Herren
Jake Harding
Lance Zarimba
Len Barot
Logan Zachary
Patricia Kendall
Sean Murray
Shawn Gadberry

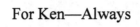

For Ken—Always

CHAPTER ONE
GOOD NIGHT, MR. RIGHT

W atch where your hands are, Ben," I warned the all-star American football player standing behind me as I slipped a key into the back door of Umberto's Salon.

"I'm afraid of the dark," Ben Pieney joked. "I need something to hold on to, Troy. Protect me."

I never thought the quarterback for the Quill Village Violators would be so frisky. To my surprise, he was all over me throughout the evening on our date. During dinner at Lassiter's Cuisine he found it necessary to stand behind me at the urinal during a restroom break and study my goods while I took a piss. And after the chick flick at the Tornado Cineplex, he shocked me with a potent tongue-kiss as his right hand unzipped a new pair of Diesel jeans. Now, as a closing to our pleasurable first date, he was about as horny as a gay seventeen-year-old at an all-male football party.

"You're so cute," he said, grinding his crotch into my bottom, wanting into my apartment above the hair salon at 2716 Manndon Street, and into my pants. "Did I tell you how much I like blonds?"

"Not recently, Ben. Why are you so bad?"

"Bad is sometimes good."

The steel door opened and a dark hallway greeted us with the raw scents of ammonia and a variety of floor cleaners. A door to the left led into my salon. At the end of the hallway was a narrow flight of stairs that welcomed very few dates to spend the night in my apartment. I walked in front of the football player. After I slipped the key into my front pocket, he gently pressed me against the closest wall at the bottom of the stairs, buried his face into my face, kissed my lips, my cheek, and my neck.

He smelled of an ash-scented soap, while he cradled my body against his large one, and proceeded with more tongue-kisses.

I had to pull away from him to stay a gentleman.

He asked, "Can you show me your upstairs?" and unbuttoned my Kenneth Cole shirt and dropped it to the hallway's oak floor.

I placed my fingers against his lips and warned, "Be careful and slow down. I'll take you on a tour of my apartment under one condition."

"What condition?"

"No frontal nudity tonight. I don't put out on the first date." It was a little white lie, but Pieney didn't need to know the truth about my dating habits. In all honesty, I hadn't had a quarterback in bed, against a wall, or over a couch since high school. Pieney was about to fill that void. There was no way I could pass up his shoulders and his green eyes. I wanted to play discreet, but not hard to get. Truth was I hadn't accomplished "the naughty" with a man in the past three months, and wanted him to roughly nail me.

"No frontal nudity?" He looked helpless.

"None. I'm not that kind of guy." Just to let him know who was boss, I teased his chest with my fingers, eventually unbuttoned his slacks and shirt, slipped a palm against his fine skin, discovered a nicely built and bare torso, and dropped the act of playing virgin boy as I fell to my knees.

❖

I knew how to treat a man with my mouth. I lathered the tip of his cock with my tongue. My fingers held the prick by its base as I consumed its length with a needy hunger. Inch after inch of the pole slid down the back of my throat. I worked on it with a steady passion.

Before he had the opportunity to blow his load in my mouth, he mumbled, "Stop, Troy," and pushed my head away.

I stood and wiped a hand over my lips. Outside my apartment's walnut door, at the top of the stairs, Ben Pieney dragged his mouth against my suntanned chest, both nipples, kissed me hard on the lips, moaned a little, and whispered, "You're a dick tease."

"Licensed and unforgettable," I said.

"Sex is a game for you, isn't it?"

"I thought you liked games?"

"On the field or off?"

"Does it matter, Ben?"

"If we're connected together, I guess it doesn't."

Okay. So the jock had me right where he wanted me. He was going to spend the night with me, or half the night; whenever I decided it was necessary to kick him out of my apartment. He was the perfect date. A guy I really didn't want to let get away, and maybe even wanted to keep for a while.

Mr. Right for all the right reasons.

I felt his breath on my neck and said, "You have to release me so we can get into my apartment."

"I'd rather get into your pants right here and right now."

I pushed his fingers away from the button and zipper on my Diesels, kissed his cheek. "You don't waste any time, do you?"

"Life is short, Troy. I believe in playing hard."

"Of course you do. What was I thinking?" I gently pulled away, found the appropriate key, and opened the door.

The Napco residence alarm system chirped and I keyed in my birth date, disabling the motion detectors. I flicked on the light. The studio was decorated by one of my dearest friends, Alonzo Filigree, a Jamaican queen who was the spitting image of Ziggy Marley. Filigree had decorated the room with topaz sofas that sat perpendicular to each other. Picasso-like paintings of teal adorned the walls. Midnight-blue vases sat on end tables matching the floor, and marble kitchen counters accented the sofas.

I spun around. Ben Pieney stood over six-three, weighed about 240 pounds, and dressed in the world's finest labels. So very hot to the touch, steamy, and big like a bulldozer.

Behind his right shoulder was a Pottery Barn mirror. The Umberto cut was to die for, just as I expected. My spirited blue eyes looked devious and hungry. A pretty-boy smile reflected innocence and sweet charm. Troy Murdock had pulled off a stunning look for yet another date.

Satisfied with my appearance, I asked, "Would you like a drink?"

He shook his head. "Let's cut to the chase."

"What kind of chase? A chaise lounge? A chase in our boxer-briefs around the apartment?"

He removed his shirt and dropped it to the floor. I scrutinized his hairy chest and massive nipples. I licked my lips and whispered, "Too hot."

❖

I gripped the sofa with all my might. I was spanked, lightly bitten, and called the nastiest names, which only made me harder. Again and again my bottom was used by his throbbing cock.

I moaned. Without my shaft even being touched, I fired a load on the back of the sofa.

"Shooting!" Ben groaned in a state of pleasure.

In one quick motion, he pulled out of me and the condom was lost on the floor.

Ben wasn't through with me, though. He leaned over my back, extended his tongue, and licked up every drop. The guy murmured with delight, spent.

❖

Minutes later, I was tucked under my shower's warm spray. Ben appeared at the curtain and asked, "Do you happen to have any room in there for me?"

"There's a fee to pay." I pulled back the Amy Butler shower curtain.

"What kind of fee?"

I showed off my soapy goods to the quarterback and said, "I need rinsed."

"Glad to help out. Let me in."

He stepped into the shower with me, applied his lips to mine yet again, gently collected me into his titanic arms, and charitably paid his fee, as promised.

❖

Around 2:13 in the morning, I said to Ben, "You don't have to leave." I didn't want to sound desperate, but I wanted to share an early Saturday-morning breakfast with him.

"I have a meeting with the coach at nine tomorrow morning. Bassett will kill me if I'm not there."

I didn't push. All the good guys in my life always seemed to meander away; apparently Pieney wouldn't be different.

"Can we go out again?" I asked.

He slipped into his Aussiebum underwear, jeans, Polo flats, and then his shirt. "I'd like that, Troy."

"Sunday night for dinner would be nice."

He nodded, ran a hand through his military cut, and said, "I'm game. Count me in."

"I can make reservations at Padlock's for eight o'clock." The queer bar and grill was the place to hang out. I knew the owner—a friend of a friend of a friend, of course—and could get us in.

"Padlock's sounds fun."

"Then off you go."

"Off I go."

"I'll walk you out."

"You're such a nice boy, Troy."

"And you're a promising poet." I slapped his bottom and walked him out of my apartment.

❖

We kissed good night in the downstairs hallway, outside Umberto's rear door. Ben said, "You know how to show a guy a good time, Charlie Brown," and breathed me in for a final time.

"Thank you, Ben."

"And we'll hook up on Sunday, right?"

"Sunday for dinner."

"I'll pick you up here at seven."

"You're such a gentleman." I closed the door behind him, turned the brass lock, and sealed me in for the night.

❖

Upstairs, tucked beneath a summer sheet, I dreamed of being on the football field at the fifty yard line with Ben. In front of him, ready for the play of our lives, I felt his strong hands on me. I heard him call out an arrangement of prime numbers. Pieney yelled, "Hike!" and I handed the football between my strong legs into his nimble hands. I blocked him from getting sacked by a fleet of boat-size Redfield Racers, listened to the crowd of forty thousand go wild as Pieney passed the ball to one of our runners and...

Chapter Two
No Longer a Hero

July 10. Saturday. Umberto Clemente's scream woke me at seven o'clock the next morning. I sat up in bed and felt my heart race with a sense of horror.

Umberto let out another scream, except this one was louder.

I bolted from the bed in my boxers, took two steps at a time on my way down, reached the bottom, and...

"I can't look, Troy! I can't look!" Umberto screamed. The drama queen hid his face in his unsteady hands. A Prada purse dangled from his right wrist.

It was a horrifying sight, maddening and distressing. Something out of a slice-and-dice film. In front of Umberto's rear door lay a naked Benjamin Pieney with his neck sliced open.

My business partner exclaimed, "I'm calling nine-one-one!"

As he phoned the Quill Village Police Department, I moved a few steps down the hallway and closer to my hero's motionless body. The slice across his neck was jagged and looked as if barbed wire had been used to mutilate Ben's thick neck. His beautiful eyes were now glassy. The quarterback's face was splattered with his own blood. His mouth was slightly open and...

"Don't touch him!" Umberto yelled, closing his Droid II and slipping it into his purse following his call to the police. "Don't even get close to him!"

I didn't. I felt dizzy and confused, and asked, "What the fuck happened?"

Umberto had beautiful skin, coconut shell–colored eyes, plump lips, and high cheekbones, and stood just over six feet tall. His taste was expensive: Prada, Diesel, Hugo Boss, Yves St. Laurent, Donna Karen, Tommy, Vestal, Cole Haan, Versace, and Miu Miu. His style was expensive and rich-looking. He considered himself one of the elite, but I knew better. His home was Quill Village, New York. And his love was Umberto's Salon at 2715 Manndon Street, our business investment that created beautiful hair in our neighborhood of NYC.

He looked helpless on the other side of the corpse. I stood by the stairs.

"What did you do to him?" he asked.

I saw the paper cup and Brogues latte at his feet. I shook my head. "It was a great date. We made plans for Sunday. What are you saying?"

"We all have bad dates, but this is ridiculous, completely uncivilized." He glanced at the cadaver again, covered his mouth, and quickly turned away.

"I locked the door after he left."

"That door wasn't locked. I didn't use my key."

"Of course you did."

"Of course I didn't. What about your shirt and shoes on the floor, Troy?"

Christ! I looked around my feet and shook my head. "It's not what it looks like."

"What does it look like, then?" he asked, studying the glass door to the salon.

"Stop thinking that way. I didn't kill him."

A Quill Village investigating detective showed up. I rolled my eyes and said, "This can't get any worse."

Zane Ward was twenty-nine years old, bald, and adorable, with amber eyes and a sexy scar along the right side of his mouth.

My history with Zane was sketchy, difficult for any sane person to digest. Not only did we attend Ruthner High School together (Ward was a jock like Ben), but we also attended Ausdbreck College at the same time, although we didn't have any classes together and seldom saw each other.

Our dating had been sporadic throughout the past year. After Zane accidentally shot me in the right foot with his Colt .45 on our first date back in November, I vowed never to see him again. I broke down and went out with him a second time in December, just before Christmas. Unfortunately, I agreed to dinner at his apartment on Broad Street. He served red bell pepper soup with lime chicken. The chicken was bad and I spent twenty-four hours on my sofa yacking my guts out. I gave in to his unlimited begging and accepted a third date, which was this past Valentine's Day. While we ice-skated at Lamley Square, enjoying a romantic song by Michael Bublé, he lost his balance, pushed me head-first to the ice, and sliced my shin open with his right skate. Approximately twelve stitches later (seven on my forehead and five on my right shin), I ditched Ward for good and vowed never to be in his company again.

I couldn't recall how many emails, tweets, voicemails, and text messages I had ignored from Detective Zane Ward. It's not that he wasn't cute and appealing for a man—regrettably, he was followed by pandemonium wherever he went.

Umberto crossed himself, looked up at the ceiling, and said, "Dear Christ, save us from the disaster that's about to happen."

Zane bowed his head, shaved approximately every two weeks by Umberto, offering a morning hello. He looked from Ben Pieney to me, back at the quarterback's body, and then at my shirt and shoes on the floor.

"Lucy," I said in my best Cuban accent, "I've got a lot of 'splaining to do."

Zane shared his upturned grin with me and said, "I'm afraid you do, Troy. So nice that we meet again."

❖

Three more officers arrived at the rear door to Umberto's Salon. The coroner, Neil Waterson, arrived with Umberto's mother, Carla Bell-Clemente. The two were dating and were sharing a Saturday-morning breakfast together at Pam's Diner when he received the call. Carla Bell-Clemente was on the plumpish side, sixtyish, with big onyx-colored hair, titanic-size lips colored Jezebel red, and a five-eight frame.

I watched Zane circle the body. He slipped on a pair of gloves, touched the body's mouth, found a yellow object inside, and pulled it free.

Mrs. Carla Bell-Clemente asked, "What is it?"

Zane was not amused and said, "Would someone please remove these people?"

We were escorted away from the crime scene, placed into the backseat of a cruiser, and taken to the precinct on Powder Street.

❖

Sixty minutes later, in an interrogation room with gray walls, a laminated table, and two chairs, Zane sat across from me and said, "Tell me what the fuck you did, Troy."

"Nice tone, Zane."

"It's my job. I need details."

"Do I look like I could murder a quarterback? The guy is more than twice my size."

"Walk me through the date."

"Which one?" I asked. "I'm particularly fond of the ice-skating incident this past February."

He sighed heavily. "That's not funny. Let's keep this about the dead hero. Now, tell me, did you lock the door behind Pieney when he left?"

I nodded and replied, "Yes. I locked the door behind him."

"And he was fully dressed?"

"Yes. Of course."

"When did he leave your flat?"

I'd already told him the answer to that question twice. I snapped, "At approximately two fifteen in the morning."

"You didn't have a fight with him, right?"

"No. It was a fun and safe date. No harm was done."

Zane didn't appreciate my answer. "You two fucked, right?"

"Yes…and we shared a shower afterward."

"Did anyone contact him while the two of you were on the date?"

"No. I was with him the entire time. It was just the two of us…You can't possibly think I'm a murderer, Zane. Come on, you know me well enough to say I wouldn't hurt a fly, let alone the sexiest quarterback in the tri-state area, minus Tom Brady, of course."

He chose not to answer.

❖

Umberto and I were still under investigation but free to go. Ben Pieney's body was whisked away. Zane's partner, Detective Nina Bowel, informed Umberto the shop would be closed for the next week (possibly even longer) while the murder investigation took place. Of course, I was not permitted in my apartment. Fortunately, Umberto had a "Princess Room" in his apartment and welcomed me to stay with him for as long as I needed.

Umberto and I walked back to his apartment on Lippincott Street. I sported a pair of snug shorts and a Nike muscle shirt that Detective Ward had rescued from my apartment, among other clothes from my drawers and closet. I asked Umberto, "What was in Ben's mouth?"

"Something yellow, I think. I'm not really sure."

"A piece of paper? A ring? What? I really didn't get to see it."

The hairdresser shook his head and replied, "Your boy Zane didn't want us to see."

"He's not my boy."

"He wants to be your boy."

"He wants a lot of things from me that he isn't going to get."

My sidekick patted me on the back and said, "Zane can't help that he is clumsy on dates."

"He almost murdered me at Lamley Square."

"What's a few stitches from a hot cop?"

I sighed heavily and decided to change the subject. "I can't stay in the Princess Room. You have a lover now. You've been waiting for a private life with Mr. Icelandic for the past three years."

"Where will you stay, then?"

We both lived in Quill Village. Beneath apartments and five-story buildings were retail stores lining the avenues and streets. We passed the local doughnut shop, two Italian restaurants, Foxy Manco's Gym, the post office, and other commercial spaces.

"I have no idea. I just don't feel right staying in the Princess Room with Axel there."

The day had started to warm and Umberto was already beginning to sweat. Wet patches of perspiration formed under his silk shirt. His voice wavered as he suggested, "My mother has a spare closet you can stay in."

"How delightful. Did Alonzo Filigree decorate it?"

"Three snaps to that," he responded. He then added something in Spanish I didn't understand but assumed was rather rude.

"I don't like living in closets. I spent the first fifteen years of my life in a closet and I don't intend to return there."

"Suit yourself, Troy."

"Thank you."

"The Princess Room awaits you, darling."

❖

In apartment E-2 on Lippincott Street, I shook Axel Bartholm's hand. I admired his spiked white hair, broad shoulders, six-four height, pink cheeks, crystal-blue eyes, and Icelandic accent. Although Axel was very bright, he spoke horrible English. Umberto did most of the translating for him.

The place was smaller than mine by a long shot. As Picasso blue as my flat was, Umberto's apartment was a shocking red; perhaps another one of Alonzo Filigree's expensive adventures in so-called decorative art. Paintings by a local impressionistic artist, Jude Mossier, hung on the walls. Imported Spanish tile decorated all the floors. A strawberry-colored settee and matching reading chairs welcomed me into a sitting room.

The kitchen had fire-hydrant-red counters, appliances, and cupboards. The bathroom—the only one in the apartment, that we would all share—was rich with maroons, scented jasmine candles, and expensive soaps.

Behind me, Umberto whispered, "Brace yourself, I've made a few changes. You're going to absolutely die when you see them."

For someone with zest and style, he had turned the room into a disaster. Red shag carpet hung on the walls. A sequined hammock decorated a nearby corner. A disco ball hung from the ceiling. And Lady Gaga posters garnished the walls.

"Oh my God," I said and stepped backward.

"Isn't it magical? A total princess's delight."

"I'm awestruck. What made you do this?"

"Axel helped me. We enjoyed a craft weekend together and…three snaps and all that…"

I spun around, placed my palms on Umberto's strong shoulders, and asked, "Can I be honest?"

"Of course, Troy. We're best friends. We never lie to each other."

"This may hurt, though."

"Bring it on. I can man it up. I'm ready for some constructive criticism."

I couldn't tell him the truth about how I felt regarding his horrendous decorating impulse. Instead, I was grateful to have a room to sleep in until Ben Pieney's murder was solved and I could be back in my apartment. I gently pulled him to me, shared a hug with the man, kissed him on the cheek in a delicate manner, and whispered into his left ear, "You're the best. This room is delightful. Thank you."

He kissed me back and smiled. "I knew you'd find it magical for your fairy needs, darling."

Chapter Three
Desperado

Tucked within dreams, I met Ben Pieney again. We shook hands, touched our chests together, and kissed. We played tackle football and fondled each other's goods under the bleachers at the fifty yard line in the Violator Stadium, showered together in the professional team's locker room, and ended up in the Princess Room's glittery hammock, side by side.

During a breakfast that consisted of Special K cereal, fresh strawberries, and a glass of orange juice, Umberto stated, "A visitor was here to see you this morning."

I looked over my sunflower-yellow Fiesta bowl. "Who?"

"I suppose it was your boyfriend."

"I don't have a boyfriend." I obviously looked puzzled and confused by his comment. He knew quite well that the last boyfriend I had was Ivan Reed, a mechanic from Sharpstown. He occasionally liked women a little more than men, something I wasn't too pleased to learn and ended up dumping him over.

"Think about it," he said over his bowl of Special K.

I shrugged and replied, "I have no idea who you're talking about."

"I'll give you three guesses and the first two don't count."

It hit me out of the blue. "Zane, right?"

"He wants you to call him. He said he needs to talk to you about Ben."

"What about Ben?" Okay, so curiosity was killing me and I wanted to know what Zane truly wanted.

"Beats me, darling. Here's his card." He passed me Zane's card across the table.

"Do you think I should call him?"

"Yes."

"Why?"

"He sounded desperate."

"All men sound desperate when they're not getting nailed in the sack."

"It wasn't like that," he said. "He needs you for something…and I'm not talking about hanky-panky stuff. It sounded like business to me."

"I'm sure he thinks I committed murder."

"How should I know?" He shrugged and waved his cereal spoon at me. "Give him a call and find out."

Approximately fifteen minutes later, I was tucked inside the Princess Room, which had a private phone line, and called Zane.

After three rings, I left the message: "I heard you wanted to speak with me. This better not be personal because I'll say no. Call me if what you need is an important business matter."

❖

I decided to visit my mother on Wilde Street. Mother Minnie lived in the Tudor-style home I grew up in, the same house where I kissed my first boyfriend, Stanley Diver, and swam buck-ass naked in our backyard pool with Justin Plural, the quarterback of our high school football team. My father had been missing since 1999 and Mother was still not over his abandonment. I felt obligated to take care of her to the best of my abilities. My straight older brother, Cody, also visited her frequently. He lived just a few blocks from Mother.

Mother was not looking like herself. She usually sported fake fingernails, layers of jewelry, three-story blond hair, and tight leopard-skin leotards. Instead, she looked bemused by my unannounced arrival, my current state of notoriety and celebrity. She stood in front of her bay window overlooking Wilde Street. Her hair was uncombed and there were dark circles under her gray eyes. She had spent all morning in front of the television watching the local news stations. "Where have you been? What's going on, Troy? It's all over the news. That poor football player was murdered in your building. He was butchered. I don't understand any of it."

"I don't either," I said, pulling away from her.

"I tried to call your cell phone a hundred times and you wouldn't pick up. I tried your apartment. I tried the salon. I even tried to reach Umberto, but he didn't pick up, either."

"Calm down," I said while retrieving two of my father's crystal rocks glasses from the bar he built in Mother's living room when I was twelve years old. I found a bottle of Jim Beam, filled both glasses halfway, and said, "Take a sip. You definitely need it."

She chugged it down in two gulps, wiped the back of her right hand across her mouth, and politely asked for more.

"Let that settle in first for a few minutes. You don't want to overdo it just yet."

"Are you safe? What did the police do to you? Where

is Umberto? What's going on? Where did you sleep last night? And why the fuck didn't you call me?" She pushed two fingertips into my right side in a motherly and playful manner.

I took a sip, then walked her through my misadventures with the professional football player, Umberto, and Detective Zane Ward.

Mother helped herself to another Beam and started pacing the room while running a hand through her unkempt hair. "Did you call Earl yet?"

"Earl Carbon, your lawyer?"

"Yes, Earl. He can help you. He's very good at what he does. You'd be blessed to have him represent you."

"Mother, I don't need a lawyer. I'm innocent. Zane knows I didn't murder Ben Pieney."

"I'll call Earl for you." She crossed the room to her Panasonic. Jim Beam sloshed out of her glass and dripped on her Berber carpet.

"You don't have to do that. I have my own lawyer. Besides, I really don't need to speak with one just yet. I'm not on a suspect list." Mother scowled at me and hissed, "You don't intend on using that lesbian woman to represent you, do you?"

"Margie Hunt is a very good lawyer. Her sexuality has nothing to do with how well she defends her clients."

"You can't trust dykes these days. Those women are brutal."

Although I considered Margaret Rachel Hunt a personal friend since high school, Mother loathed her and blamed her for somehow morphing me into a gay man. I said, "Can I spend a few nights with you?"

"You can't, honey. I've been very busy."

"Not even one night?"

"I'm afraid not. The bedrooms are covered in aluminum pillows."

"Not again." I picked up my Beam and downed half of it. "Tell me you're not trying the Andy Warhol thing for a second time."

"It's my third try," Mother informed me. "Not that it's any of your business, Troy. I'm not going to stop until it's just right."

"Shit," I said. "You'll go mad trying to do the Warhol thing."

"Watch your language in my house."

Mother's infatuation with Andy Warhol was unending. Not only did she collect empty tomato soup cans and department store shoe ads, but she also built her own electric chair in the basement. Cody had refused to install the 220 line during his senior year of college for it to work—Thank Jesus! Throughout the years she'd tried silk-screening, traveled around the city taking photographs of car wrecks, and experimented with other Warhol techniques. In the past two years she had visited the artist's museum in Pittsburgh over twenty times. Upon each visit she became totally infatuated with that ridiculous room filled with the aluminum-colored helium pillows that floated in circles with the help of a fan. She wanted to create that same room in her house. Unfortunately, the aluminum foil–covered balloons, or "pillows" as she referred to them, exploded or deflated by mid-project and she had to start her task over from scratch. Like Warhol, she didn't give up, didn't care what people thought, and would continue until she felt she had mastered it.

"Can I sleep on the couch?"

"You can't. That's my thinking place."

Her phone rang and she picked it up. "Hello?" she

singsonged into the phone, and smiled. She pulled the phone away from her ear and said to me, "It's Earl Carbon. Isn't that a coincidence?"

Quickly, I chugged the last of my Jim Beam and bolted from her house.

Of course, I was desperate for a place to stay for the next few nights. The last thing I really wanted to do was stay at Umberto's. While driving my Jeep Wrangler away from my partner's pad, I'd thought about calling up the employees of Umberto's Salon to see if I could spend a few nights at one of their comfy and available abodes. To no avail. In the end, I was stuck staying in the Princess Room.

❖

After I pulled into a parking spot in front of Umberto's apartment building, my cell phone rang.

"Troy?" It was Zane, just as I had expected.

"Long time no talk."

"This is serious. I really want to speak with you if you have the time. Is it possible to meet you somewhere?"

I replied, "Only if you don't try to kill me during one of your accidents."

Silence.

"Are you there, Zane? Did I lose you?" I asked.

"I'm here."

"I could use a cup of coffee. Would you like to meet at Delia's in fifteen minutes?"

"I'll be there."

Delia's Danish Delights was located on the corner of Brighton and Smithton. Zane was seated next to the sidewalk, discreetly shaded by a green-and-white umbrella at a round table. He had a tall, plain coffee in front of him on a Delia's napkin. He was apparently off duty because he was out of his crisp uniform and sporting a pair of Energie khaki shorts and a red, white, and blue plaid cotton shirt. After a sweet handshake and a generous smile, he said, "I've taken the liberty of ordering for you. My treat."

I sat down across from him at the four-person table and picked up the tall caramel latte. I swallowed a mouthful and responded with, "You remembered what I like. Thank you."

"I did. It's the least I can do for meeting me on such short notice. By the way, thanks for coming."

"Of course."

"I want to help you, Troy."

"How so?"

"The only reason you're not behind bars for Benjamin Pieney's murder is because of me." He sipped his coffee, swallowed, and added, "Over half the city thinks you murdered our hometown hero."

I shook my head and cleared my throat. "There is no way I could pull off a murder like that. Something was shoved down his throat and...and I can't even prepare fresh fish from Marcelo's Market, let alone slice open a quarterback's throat."

"I know. That's why I want to help you."

"You know I'm innocent?" I sounded pathetic.

He nodded. "I never doubted you for a second. I'm going with my heart on this—you were not capable of killing your boyfriend."

I waved a hand and corrected him. "He wasn't my boyfriend. It was our first date."

"How long did you know him?"

"Everyone knows Ben Pieney. He took our city to the Titan Bowl last year. He's famous around the country. People love him. Fans want to be kissed by him. Football players are jealous of his career."

"I mean personally and intimately?"

"Less than a month. Umberto trimmed his hair three weeks in a row. I guess Ben was sort of stalking me at the shop, liked what he saw, and eventually found the guts to ask me out on a date. I accepted. It was nothing shocking."

"When did he ask you out?"

"This past Tuesday." I paused, studied the other coffee drinkers, and inquired, "How is this going to help me?"

He sat back in his chair, crossed his palms over his hulking chest, and drew his fingers together in a churchlike structure. "Where are you staying?"

"In the Princess Room."

"Where the fuck is that?"

"In Umberto's apartment. It's horribly pink and feminine."

"I would have thought you would like that."

I took another sip of my latte and said, "I don't like listening to Umberto and his Icelandic lover fuck. In truth, I find it rather repulsive and daunting. I'm going to need lots of therapy."

Zane smiled and said, "I want your help with this case, Troy."

"I run a hair business. I don't do murder cases. Besides, you always want things from me, but that doesn't mean you can get them."

"I have to keep a close eye on you."

"Why?"

"Because I want you to stay safe. Something tells me you're in danger."

"I'm only in danger in your presence. Let me remind you

how many times you tried to kill me. Besides, I didn't kill Ben. You said you believed I was innocent. Why do you need to keep me safe?"

"I have a bad feeling about this case and your involvement."

"This is bullshit," I said. "I don't need to be watched. I certainly don't need to be a part of your case…and I really don't want anything to do with you. Our days of dating are over, thanks to your skating fiasco in February."

He ignored me. "Help me, Troy. That's all I'm asking."

"You sound desperate. I don't like guys who sound or act desperate. It's creepy to hear you like that."

I stood and started walking away.

He was right beside me within seconds, handing me a card. I didn't look at it.

"I need your help on this case."

"You need nothing from me." I pulled away.

"You have to listen to me for your own good."

"You had your chance. My dates with you were nothing less than attempted murder…three times, mind you."

"This isn't about us. This is about a murder you can easily be charged for."

I stopped. "What are you saying?"

"I'm your salvation. The guy who is going to save your ass. I have your back, and I intend to look out for your safety and protect you."

I rolled my eyes. "How so?"

"You don't get how serious this is, do you?"

"Bugger off," I said. "You sound ridiculous."

"Listen to me, Troy…I'm the one keeping your ass out of jail. Do you understand that?"

"For God's sake, I didn't kill anyone. If you think I'm guilty, cuff me now. If you don't, then leave me alone."

"I know you didn't kill the superstar. Why do you think I'm here talking to you right now?"

"Because you want me back. Three dangerous dates with you wasn't good enough, and now you want a fourth."

He shook his head and sighed heavily. "Our dates have nothing to do with why I'm trying to save your ass."

"I don't believe you."

"Believe this, Troy...if you don't work with me on this case, my supervisors will have you behind bars."

"Are you blackmailing me?"

"Absolutely not."

"Then what are you saying?"

"Work with me. Help me figure out who killed Ben Pieney. And let me protect you."

I shook my head. "Absolutely not. I have better things to do with my time. I have a hair salon to run. I have men to date. I have..."

As I walked away, Zane called out behind me, "I'll give you twenty-four hours to think about it, pal! If you change your mind, call the number on the card I gave you!"

CHAPTER FOUR
THE PHOENIX IS RISING

H e wants you to do what?" Umberto was sunbathing in a Strathwood lounge chair on his outside deck. He wore a pair of boxer-briefs. The day was brilliant with astonishing rays and no wind, perfect for our company.

We were sharing a liquid lunch consisting of Long Island iced teas—which Mr. Icelandic had a knack for making. "Zane wants me to be his sidekick, to help him investigate Ben's death."

"Does he remember that he almost killed you three times?" Umberto turned on his stomach, kicked off the Mr. Turtles, and was now sunbathing nude.

"He's very aware of our past."

"Let me get this straight. After all the crazy shit with him, he still wants you to be his little investigative assistant?"

"There's nothing little about me at all, remember?"

He giggled like a boy and eventually said, "I forgot about your problem."

"It's not a problem. All the guys I sleep with enjoy my super-size meal. They like the XXX-size stuff."

The Cuban flipped over on his back. He placed his palms behind his head and glistened in the afternoon sun. "You are not my type, anyway."

"I'm not easy. You like easy men. I have a little more class than you do."

"You were easy with Ben. The man had you in his hands and you let him—"

I cut him off. "Yes, I became easy because of him. He had me in bed as soon as we met at the restaurant for dinner. What can I say? I have a weakness for all-American quarterbacks. Who doesn't?"

"Was he good in bed?"

"The best. Not too slow. Not too rough. I had fun with him." I sighed pleasantly, heavenly. This was the life. Drinks with friends, warm bare bottoms, and a sporty sun hanging over the city. Life was not going to get any better, I knew.

"Now he's gone, isn't he? The all-star players always get away, don't they?"

I sighed heavily, took another drink, closed my eyes, and asked, "Should I help Zane Ward out or not?"

"The prick in me says to tell him to fuck off."

"I already did that…twice."

"You didn't?"

"He was being atrocious."

"Most men are, even the sexy ones," he said. "Maybe you should wait it out and see what he does. If he's so desperate for your help, he'll come around again."

"What if I sleep with him? You know I have a weakness for men in uniform." We hadn't slept together. I'd calculated that sex with him was far too dangerous, given my random injuries on our previous dates. Of course I wanted to sleep with him. Two remaining questions seemed to linger within my mind, though: Was I ready to open up to the man and share a sleepover with him? Did I want to nail Zane the same way he maybe wanted to nail me?

"Then something else will be coming, darling."

"I mean...what if I do end up helping him and he uses his bedroom eyes on me? The guy is dreamy for all the right reasons."

"Don't forget that he tried to kill you three times, Troy."

"Accidentally."

"Yes, accidentally. It's still not the way to try and get in a detective's pants."

"I'm quite sure it's worked for many men."

"You're a whore," he said, joking.

"I forgot about that. Thanks for reminding me."

"Now, tell me why you're single."

"Because Ivan Reed got away."

"Because he liked pussy. I've told you not to be hard on yourself regarding him. It was something you had no control of."

"I thought my cock would keep him around."

"For about eight months, if I remember correctly."

"Nine months, one week, and four days, if you want to know the truth."

He giggled and said, "You are still hard for him, aren't you?"

"I fell in love with Ivan. He broke my heart."

"We can always get you a sex change and breast implants, darling."

"Bugger off, Umberto."

"You're so dramatic. I was just kidding. Now, back to Ward. What are you going to do with him? Will you play or not?"

"I don't know yet."

"Mother Umberto suggests riding it out. Let him beg for your help and sex."

"He's practically done that."

"Let him beg more."

"Umberto, you know I hate desperate men."

"It's not about finding him desperate, Troy. It's about payback."

"Payback? What are you talking about?"

"He owes you, darling. Zane not only shot and poisoned you, he sliced your leg open with an ice skate. It's time for some payback. Let him struggle a bit."

"I will not sleep with him," I said. "That's an injury just waiting to happen."

"Did I say anything about a bed companion?"

"No."

"Of course I didn't," he said. "Now, let him struggle a bit and you take baby steps in this matter. I'm sure by then you will know exactly what to do."

"Love him or leave him."

"Exactly."

I moved my Long Island to his, clinked the glasses together, and said, "Cheers."

"Cheers, my friend."

For the next twenty minutes we drank and baked under the sun. He shared gossip with me regarding our staff at the salon. I explained Mother's Andy Warhol phase again with the aluminum pillows and...

❖

The Icelandic bobsledder had an American friend named Timothy Mantra who happened to be a semi-famous artist in Quill Village. Mantra had an opening for his clay and plastic pieces of art at the Bostin-Gallic Gallery on Sutner Street. Axel was taking Umberto as his date, and to meet Mantra.

I had Umberto's apartment to myself and decided to take

the evening off, watch a movie called *Loggerheads*, catch up on my reading, and maybe digest a few extra calories. Umberto and Axel were not due in until one or two in the morning, which left me plenty of time for a long bath, the newest Ben Tyler novel, and chamomile suds up to my jaws.

Unfortunately, Mother called and interrupted my undressing. I snatched up my cell and barked, "Yes?"

"You're using that disrespectful tone with me again, Troy Murdock. What have I told you about that?"

"I'm sorry. I was just getting ready to slip into the tub."

"Then my news about Blaine Phoenix will hold no interest for you."

"Who is Blaine Phoenix, and why would I have an interest in him?"

Silence. I waited for her to respond, which she didn't, and I asked, "Are you there?"

"I'm here. I just heard something strange outside. A garbage can being hit or something like that."

"Is Mr. Obner home?" Since my father's disappearance, Mr. Obner watched out for Mother's safety. The ex-Marine was still bulky at sixty-five, could throw a nasty punch at an uninvited intruder, and knew how to shoot a gun, if necessary.

"Yes. I think."

"Are his lights on?"

She paused. I imagined her looking out her kitchen window, straining her neck with wide eyes and one hand on her hip. Eventually, she answered, "They are."

"Don't be afraid to use him if you have to."

"I won't, Troy. I'm sure it was just a cat getting to fish bones or something like that." She asked, "Don't you want to hear about Blaine Phoenix?"

Not exactly. I wanted to slip into bubbles and pass a

good hour in seclusion. "Hit me," I said, pushing Mother into speaking faster so I could get down to my bathroom business.

"He's a friend of that Ben Pieney's."

"How were they friends?" I asked, a little taken aback What was their connection?

"I have no idea. Do I look like I work for the *QV Tattler*?"

"Of course not, Mother. What did this guy Blaine want?"

Nonchalantly, she said, "He stopped by here and wanted to know how you knew Ben, and for how long. He asked about Umberto's, how long you two owned the hair salon, and a few other questions."

I started to panic and gasped a little. "Did you tell him where I was staying?"

"Yes, of course. He seemed like a very nice young man. Big like our hero Ben. Red hair with squinty eyes. A very handsome man with one of those furry devils on his chin."

Shit! I thought. "What else did he want?"

"He wanted to know what you were driving."

"I assume you told him?"

"Yes, of course. I told you he was nice."

I tried to make a joke, "Jeffrey Dahmer was nice, too, Mother," but it went over her head. I asked, "What was he driving, Mother?"

"I don't know."

"What color was it?"

"Black...and sporty-looking."

I listened to her breathing, heard aluminum crinkling in the background, and then Mother said, "Mrs. Hark's cats are at it again. They love my garbage. I threw some tuna fish cans away today and they're on a mission to find them."

Better the cats than the mysterious Blaine Phoenix bothering my mother, I rationalized.

"Sweetie, I have to go. I'm going after the cats."

"Be careful, Mother."

"Always," she whispered. "I'm old enough to take care of myself."

Before ending the call, I said, "Sometimes I wonder about that," and meant it.

❖

I had to relax, calm down, and find my Zen while Umberto and Axel were out. After fully undressing and filling the tub with warm water and suds, I climbed inside with Mr. Tyler's *One Night Stand*, and started reading.

Not a minute later I heard someone knock on the front door of Umberto's apartment. I tried to ignore the interruption and continued to read. The knocking grew louder and most bothersome. I slammed the book closed, stood in the tub, and yelled, "I'm coming! Hold your nuts on!"

After I slipped a mauve-colored towel around my waist, I made my way out of the bathroom. As the knocking continued, I screamed with disgust, "Give me a fucking minute!" I unlocked the three Yale locks, pulled the door open…and just about went straight.

"I need to talk to you, Troy." A flustered-looking Ivan Reed stepped into the apartment and sat down on Umberto's leather sofa.

I closed the door, held the towel to my hips so it wouldn't fall. "How did you find me?"

"Everyone knows you're staying here. It's no secret. It's all over the news since you murdered the quarterback."

"I didn't murder Ben," I snapped. "Now that we have that clear, what do you want?"

"Advice. You were always good at giving advice."

Ivan looked as adorable as when we were seeing each other. His blue eyes melted me and his pouty lips desired nothing less than a kiss from me. He had dark skin like his Italian mother, a firm jaw, wide shoulders, and a tough-looking chest, just like his father, Timothy Reed. In truth, I had missed him dearly and wished he was holding me instead of the waitress at Hooter's that he fell for and…

"Someone's following me," Ivan said.

"Who and why?" I asked, sitting down beside him in the towel, dripping wet.

"I don't know. Some big guy with a black Mustang and a red goatee."

His brief description matched Mother's uninvited guest, Blaine Phoenix. "Where were you when you first saw him?"

"At my apartment with Luanne." Luanne Pringle was the big-breasted Hooter's waitress who'd whisked Ivan away from me and ruined our relationship.

"How did you see him?"

"My apartment's on the first floor, and you can see everyone walk past. I saw him a few times. Then he was following me in his Mustang to the bookstore yesterday, MacField's Food Mart this morning, and…"

"Did he follow you here?" I asked.

"I don't know. I don't think so, but I'm not sure."

I started to panic, placed my hand on his right shoulder, and said, "You look pale. Do you need a drink?"

Ivan nodded and asked for white wine.

I stood and said, "Let me find some." As I walked away the towel dropped to my feet and accidentally showed my ass off to my ex-boyfriend. Embarrassed, I rewrapped it around my waist and apologized.

"It's not a bad-looking ass, Troy. You should show it off more."

I headed for the kitchen, found two glasses and a bottle of cheap wine, and went back into the living room.

❖

I was not in love with Ivan Reed anymore, honestly; or at least I tried to convince myself of that. No longer did we share the same apartment on Stewart Way. No longer did we eat breakfast and dinner together. No longer did we have plans to retire in Ogunquit, Maine. Our lives were shattered because of his straying. He now had his own life and I had mine. If we were any more separated, we'd be living in different states.

I passed him a glass of wine and asked, "Can you give me more information about this Mustang-driving stalker?"

Ivan said, "I never said he was a stalker. I merely said he was following me."

"Did he try to hurt you?"

"Not that I'm aware of."

"No guns, knives, or nuclear weapons?"

"Nuclear weapons? What do you mean by that, Troy?"

"Never mind. It was a joke. Any guns or knives that you saw?"

"He's not a criminal. He's just a follower, lurker, or watcher. Whatever you want to call him."

I ignored his comment and proceeded with my inquiry. "Was he alone?"

"Well, I think he was alone. I didn't see anyone with him."

"No one in the passenger seat of his Mustang?"

"I can't recall."

"No one on the sidewalk in front of your apartment?"

"No." He shared a direct response with me for the first time and shook his head.

"Has he been following Luanne?"

"I haven't asked her."

"Why haven't you asked her?"

"Because Luanne works all the time at Hooter's. We never see each other."

I didn't want to get personal. The less I knew about his life with Luanne, the better off I was. In truth, I just wanted to find information about Blaine Phoenix and escort Ivan Reed out of my life again. "Anything else you can share with me?"

He shrugged his shoulders in a boyish manner that was strikingly cute. I looked away from him, found my wine, consumed two gulps, swallowed, and directed my attention back to him. "Do you think your follower has a connection to Ben's death?"

"Who's Ben?"

Ivan was so cute and dumb. I rolled my eyes and said, "Ben Pieney, the quarterback for the Violators. Do you think your follower is connected to his murder?"

He said he didn't know.

"Why did you come here and find me?" I asked.

"Because I didn't know who else to tell. Luanne is at work. My brother is at his poker game tonight. Uncle Bert is in Sarasota, Florida, visiting his ex-wife. You're the only one available."

"Fourth in line. That's good to know," I said.

"What do you mean by that?"

"Don't worry about it. You have to promise me something, though."

"What?" he asked with wide eyes.

"If you see this guy again, call me. I want to know about it."

Ivan agreed and I hinted that he should leave.

CHAPTER FIVE
ARE YOU DECENT, MR. MURDOCK?

Umberto called around one o'clock in the morning and woke me from a dream that consisted of two naked blonds who just happened to be underwear models for International Male. The Cuban slurred my name into the phone, giggled, and asked, "Are you naked, dumpling?"

"Have you been drinking?" I groggily asked, rubbing a fist in my right eye.

"A little." He hiccupped, which I found adorable.

"Are you drunk, Umberto?"

"A lot." He laughed, snorting like a pig.

"Is Axel with you?"

"The man is on his knees right now, waiting for some naughty."

"Do you two need a ride home? I don't want either of you to drive while intoxicated. A taxi is cheaper than a DUI fine."

He slurred, "We're staying overnight at the Hilton. Paris is going to make a sex tape with us and share a line of her cocaine."

I played along. "I'll buy it when it comes out on DVD. As for the cocaine, stay away from the shit. It will kill you."

"She's calling for me now, dumpling. I have to run."

He ended the call with inebriated glee in his voice. I drifted off to sleep with a smile on my face and an immediate dream of shopping in Beverly Hills.

Just as I was about to try on a rainbow-colored taffeta dress with shoulder pads and a pair of Corks boots, I was whisked out of the Paris Hilton dream by the portable pink phone in the Princess Room.

In a severe state of grogginess, I picked up the phone, cleared my throat, wiped my nose, and mumbled, "What?" into the receiver.

"Troy?" The voice sounded brisk and cold.

"Ivan, is that you?"

"No."

"Who is this?"

"Someone who just happens to be watching you."

I sat up in the pink bed, felt shivers at my spine, cleared my throat for a second time, and asked, "Who the fuck is this?"

Dead silence. Nothing. No one.

"Hello?" I asked, thinking I'd lost them.

"I'm here."

"Is this Blaine Phoenix?"

Again, I heard nothing.

"Blaine, is that you? What do you want with me? What's going on? What are you calling me for?"

I heard a click and then a steady dial tone. Feeling jittery, unable to sleep, I didn't know what to do. Half of me wanted to call Zane. The other half of me wanted to ignore the disturbance and go back to sleep.

Fortunately, the later idea panned out after a glass of warm milk in the kitchen. Once back in bed I drifted off to sleep.

❖

Ever since I was a child I've sleepwalked. Mother was always pulling me out of the refrigerator, garage, or doghouse at four o'clock in the morning. I walked through the house like a zombie, found the television set and climbed behind it, discovered a closet and hid inside it until dawn, or meandered into the backyard and climbed into the sandbox. Unfortunately, in my adulthood, I was still not cured.

There were only four people who knew about my sleepwalking condition: Mother, Father, my brother Cody, and Ivan Reed. If Zane or a fellow officer of the law got wind of it, they'd throw me behind bars for sure, accusing me of murder. I made certain they didn't know, and had definitely fretted over falling asleep and doing something stupid following Ben's murder.

The bedroom windows and door of the Princess Room were locked; better safe than sorry. I was exhausted, stressed over Ben's murder. I had selfishly planned on sleeping straight through the night without any interruptions, such as sleepwalking or answering the phone.

That second night at Umberto's place, I didn't dream of shopping. Instead, my sleepwalking returned. I climbed out of bed, exited the Princess Room, and found myself in Umberto's living room, buck-naked and with a can of Diet Pepsi positioned at my lips, comfortable on his Belgian sofa.

What woke me was nothing laughable. I smelled smoke and rubber burning and heard the Quill Village Fire Department sirens screaming throughout the neighborhood. Someone banged on the apartment door and hollered something unintelligible.

I came to, dropped the can of Diet Pepsi to the floor at my feet, blinked a few times, and noticed I was naked.

On the opposite side of the apartment's closed and locked door, Mr. Tibet—a sixty-three-year-old editor for Penderton

Books, and a close friend to Umberto—stood in the hallway and banged his fist on the wooden plane. He screamed, "It's your Jeep, Troy! Your Jeep is on fire!"

I was wide awake now, and dashed around the sofa to a living room window. In the parking lot, next to the apartment building, I saw flames shooting out of my 2007 Jeep's windows. I had just paid the damn thing off in full a month before. I swore at the window.

Again, Mr. Tibet banged a fist on the apartment's door, this time harder and with more concern. "Are you in there, Troy?"

"I'm here, Mr. Tibet!"

"You'd better come out! The QVFD is here, and—and the PD was called!"

Christ, just what I needed. I yelled, "I'll be out in a second!" and dashed off to the Princess Room where I put on white boxer briefs and a pair of summer shorts and slipped my feet into sandals. There was no time to fix my hair or throw a shirt on. Before I knew it, I was out in the hallway with Mr. Tibet and asked, "What's going on? What happened to my Jeep?"

James Tibet was still handsome for his age with a handlebar mustache, expressive, almost amethyst-colored eyes, rosy cheeks, and a full head of silver hair. His response was blunt and to the point. "How am I supposed to know? It's your Jeep!"

Who set my Jeep on fire, and why? Could I have discreetly escaped Umberto's pad, found my way into the parking lot, and torched one of my prized possessions? I pushed the thought far away from my mind and walked with Mr. Tibet down the flight of stairs and outside just as Zane pulled up in his green-and-white cruiser.

The Quill Village Fire Department was in the process of

putting out the fire. A strong gasoline smell wafted through the air as Zane asked, "Trouble is following you everywhere, isn't it, pal?"

I saw Mr. Tibet and other apartment tenants in a circle. I said, "I don't know what's going on in my life. The unplanned dramas are certainly out of control."

Zane licked his upper lip and teased me. "It's nice to see you dressed for the occasion."

I said sarcastically, "It's not a weenie roast. Tell me what's going on."

"By the smell of it, someone torched your Jeep with gasoline, buddy." He gently patted my chest with an outstretched palm, grasped one of my pecs, and gave it a light squeeze.

The hand felt tender against my skin, but I pulled away for fear I would end up kissing his handsome face. I said, "I think someone's out to get me."

"How many enemies do you have?" He drew his interest away from the fire and his police reports. The guy had the memory of a genius and could recall minute details of the most detailed crimes; he was a whiz at his job, the best of the best on his force at Precinct 29.

As we stood and watched the flames and firemen at work, I counted at least six enemies from the past year. There was Inna Welsh, a client with ugly hair and my endless lawsuit over her bad split ends; I constantly hassled Billy Castoratti at the butcher shop because he could never produce a flawless slab of beef for me; last summer I'd dated a guy by the name of Drake Pinnacle who considered me a bad time; Rizzi Papoli, Umberto's bitchy salon competitor, operated his business across town, Two Snips Shy; I couldn't leave out Olivia Iva because I'd "accidentally" slept with her husband, who didn't tell me he was married; my strange affair with Davy Hinder—a professor at West Quill College—was rather unkind due to his almost-fatal attraction to me after a freshman year of innocent lust and abounding erections. Yes, I had a few enemies. But who didn't, right? Life was about good and bad, and mixing it up. Love and hate stuff. Everyone I knew had enemies.

I rattled those familiar names off to Zane and said, "Not everyone's perfect."

"Trust me, you're perfect." He shared a little wink and a perfect smile.

"Are you flirting with me, Zane?"

"Absolutely not. That would be unprofessional."

"I don't believe you." The Jeep was hosed down by two hot firemen. I ogled the calendar darlings (Mr. July and Mr. September) in motion, and felt uncomfortable as Zane moved closer to me. I asked, "Do you think this fire is connected to Pieney's death?"

"One hundred percent. Nothing is a coincidence when crime is involved."

"Who's after me?" I felt his shoulder next to mine and realized that he had definitely crossed a comfort zone between us. Any closer and we would have been on our fourth date.

"That's still a mystery to me. I spoke to Ben's mother today. She's a lovely woman who seems severely heartbroken. She was so upset she couldn't even remember her son's friends' names."

"No help at all, then?" I said.

"None. Sometimes close relatives and friends will freeze up during questioning after a murder. It's normal behavior following such a shock."

I told Zane about Ivan's visit and Blaine Phoenix's antics.

"I already talked to Blaine. He was a little strange, and

hardly helpful. I sensed he was protective of his pal. Maybe football players have a secret pact regarding silence or something like that, I'm not sure. If I didn't know any better, I'd say they were lovers."

"What do you think Blaine wants with me?"

"Answers about Ben's murder. Just like everyone else in Quill Village. A hero in this city was murdered." He was quiet for a second, caught me studying Mr. September at work. "You really like guys in uniform, don't you?"

Weakly, I said, "Uniformed men are my favorite. What can I say, the whore comes out in me."

"I have a uniform to wear for you."

"I gave up detectives after you. I'm not a cat with nine lives."

"What a pity," he said. "I was hoping we could have another date and maybe talk about this fire. And if we just happened to end up in bed together…that would rock both of our worlds."

"Never." I shook my head in a vehement manner. "I have bigger things to worry about. No place to live. No vehicle. My life doesn't need a guy like you in it unless I want to die."

"A guy like me could make you happy. I would take care of you in a minute. Monetarily. Affectionately. However you would want me to. Don't forget that."

"A guy like you tried to kill me three times. You're a very dangerous man, and I'm not talking about with your cock. That's probably the only thing that doesn't scare me about you."

"You always have to bring up the petty shit, don't you."

I felt it was a good time to change the subject and mention the yellow object in Ben's mouth. Why not? What did I have to lose? I took a deep breath and inquired, "What was in Ben's mouth?"

"What's in it for me if I tell you?" Kisses were out of the question. So was a night in his arms on his waterbed.

"A pizza and six-pack of beer at your house, tomorrow evening. We can call it a dinner date, if you want. I'll bring the eats and drinks, and you pay me with your knowledge."

He nodded. "I like where you're going with this."

"There will be no kinky stuff, though. No dick teasing. No ass-handling. Nothing like that. I don't even want you to kiss me. You'll be a complete gentleman. Don't even think I'm coming over to get frisky with you. That isn't happening."

"Too bad," he said, shrugged, and raised his adorable eyebrows. "A man's got to do what a man's got to do sometimes."

"I'm coming for information and nothing more."

"Sounds fair to me. I will put more on the table if you want it."

I turned from the torched Jeep and started to walk back into the apartment building. Zane caught up to me and grasped my left shoulder. "Thanks for not wearing a T-shirt."

"My pleasure," exited my mouth without a single thought.

He cocked his head to the left. "Are you flirting with me?"

"Never." I held my ground. In a matter of seconds, I vanished from his side and headed back to bed.

Alone.

❖

Mr. Tibet, who lived across the hall, insisted I not spend the night by myself. "It's not safe, Troy. You need protection. I have a spare room you can have for the night. The last thing we need is another emergency on this block."

Of course I accepted his offer. Besides, he seemed like a harmless older gentleman. One who cared about young men such as me and my uncertain safety.

Before we turned in for the night he served me two homemade sugar cookies with lemon-flavored icing and a large glass of soy milk. Sitting across from me at a walnut table in his seventies-style kitchenette, he asked, "Who was that beefy detective you were talking with?"

"You don't want to know." I nibbled at a cookie and washed it down with a swig of milk.

"But I do. It's the least you can do for an old man who hasn't been laid in seventeen years."

"His name is Detective Zane Ward. He's an old boyfriend of mine who tried to kill me three times—unintentionally, of course."

"What a fine catch. Darling to the core. Delicious for all the right reasons. Nice to look at. All smiles. He made me hard." A soft giggle surfaced from his mouth and then he licked his lips in an act of hungry zeal.

I about choked on a mouthful of soy milk, swallowed it quickly, coughed once, and said, "He's not all that. He's an attempted murderer. A rough detective who sometimes likes to get off on beating the shit out of people."

He demanded to hear how my old boyfriend was a nuisance in my life, with no detail spared, of course.

Before I knew it, I'd rehashed my months with Detective Ward, which included bad dates, smooth kisses, and an opened book of Troy's Secret Life.

"No matter what his downfalls are, he still sounds darling. I can see it in your eyes that you like him, Troy. The eyes never lie. You do know that, don't you?"

"I'm very tired. My eyes are not functioning correctly at the moment. I'm sure you're misreading them," I said.

The editor waved a hand at me and said with a giggle, "You're a damsel in distress, darling. He's your hero. That man is going to save your life one of these days. And when he does…let him."

"I tend to disagree with you. Besides, I'm not a big believer in fortunetelling."

"Sometimes, darling, you have to take what you can get in life. If not, the door of opportunity may never open again." The older man closed his eyes and bowed his head like a wise soothsayer.

With that said, I thanked my host for his kindness in letting me spend the night with him.

❖

Mr. Tibet's spare room was small and cozy, rustic with brown and black hues, and provided a single window to observe the busy city from. Above the full-size bed was a velvet picture of Elvis in a white jumpsuit. I was not into velvet or Elvis, but sort of found the picture warmly pleasant, just like the room. PartyLite sconces hung on both sides of the picture and filled the room with a ginger scent and…

Tap. Tap. Tap.

Mr. Tibet's voice echoed dully through the door: "Are you decent, Mr. Murdock?"

I turned my attention away from Elvis, trotted across the room, and opened the door. The aged editor stood in the narrow hallway in a silk kimono covered in red and white dragons. He held a bamboo tray, which he passed to me, and said, "These things will make you comfortable during your short stay."

I politely took the tray and admired the items: a cotton towel, unopened toothbrush and toothpaste, a brand-new razor, a shot glass–sized bowl for a needed nightcap, a tiny bottle of sake, and two Red Hot condoms with a travel-sized tube of water-resistant lube. Kindly, I said, "Thank you, Mr. Tibet," and decided it was best not to mention the condoms and lube.

"Enough with the manners, my boy. Call me James."

"Thank you, James."

"A very good start between us, chap. Perhaps I'll visit you later." He cordially winked, turned away, and vanished down the hallway to his own room.

❖

I admit today, the sake went down velvety and fast following James Tibet's visit. A numb and relaxed sensation flowed through my body. I stripped out of my clothes, except for a pair of tight boxer-briefs, which I decided to wear to bed in case my host showed up in the early-morning hours and slipped into the twin bed with me.

I fell asleep, unvisited and untouched by Mr. Tibet throughout that peculiar night. There, I dreamed of another shopping spree: handbags, high heels, and scarves. I visited Ben Pieney at Quill Village Stadium, watched him practice with his sexy teammates, enjoyed the sights, and carried out a little more shopping: cosmetics, jewelry, and hats.

The next morning, Mr. Tibet prepared breakfast in bed for me: French toast, plump fingerlike sausages, and a glass of freshly squeezed orange juice. Beside my glass of juice sat a copy of the *Village Caller*. As James opened the blinds and windows in the spare room, I began to eat a link of sausage and read the front page's headline: CUTIE PIE MUST DIE!

Midway through the article about Benjamin Pieney's mysterious death, Mr. Tibet slid up to my side, observed me reading, and said, "It's a disturbing story. A yellow lapel pin was found in Ben's mouth. The pin read those revolting words: *Cutie Pie Must Die!*"

No longer was I hungry as I read the article. A sour feeling found its way inside my stomach. I sighed and said, "I've been mentioned as a key suspect."

"Umberto has too." He patted my leg underneath the summer sheet. "That doesn't mean you two are guilty, though. Both of you are upstanding citizens and neither of you would ever commit murder."

"It's an outrage," I said. "It's a witch hunt. Shame on them for pointing fingers."

My host snatched the newspaper from me and set it aside. "Better to keep your mind and nose clean, chap. There's no reason to get upset. People of Quill Village are going to think what they want to think. Don't mind them. Ben's murderer will be found. Give Zane Ward some credit."

"It's slander," I said, disgruntled and upset.

"We have other things to discuss." After he removed the almost-untouched breakfast tray from my middle, he sat on the edge of the bed next to me, patted my bare stomach, and said, "I have transportation for you, young man."

"What are you talking about?"

"My '88 Buick. I keep it parked at my sister's place in Dunshire. It's far too expensive for me to park here in the city. The car works like a gem. It's something you can rely on."

Dunshire was in New Jersey, next to Trenton. A rough little town with a lot of bad attitude, guns, prostitutes, thugs, and numerous drugs. "I can't get out to Dunshire."

"Sissy's driving the Buick here. I've already arranged it for you. She'll be arriving sometime around noon today."

"You shouldn't have," I said.

"You're absolutely right, I shouldn't have. You're an angel

to me, though. You make me feel young and handsome. It's the least I can do for you."

"I'm glad I can help," I said, deciding to eat after all, and asked for the breakfast tray back. Once he placed the tray in front of me, I slipped the end of a sausage link between my lips and nibbled a bite off.

He began to walk away from my side. Over his right shoulder, he said, "You eat your breakfast, shower, and try to relax. Before you know it, Sissy will be here with the Buick. I have a few things to do in the meantime. Cleaning. Errands. Grocery shopping. Just make yourself at home."

I nodded a greasy smile and said, "Thank you." Then I chewed up the sausage in the left side of my mouth, swallowed it down, and felt it soothe my stomach.

CHAPTER SIX
THE STRAIGHT BEAR

S ome maniac is trying to kill you, Troy." Umberto was outraged when he learned about my torched Jeep. We sat with Axel inside my business partner's kitchen. "It's ludicrous to think you're a murderer! It's turning into a nuisance. And that yellow lapel pin inside Pieney's mouth is the craziest thing I've ever heard."

"I'm going to talk to Zane this morning and get involved. I want to see if I can help in any way, since Ben's murder seems to be revolving around me."

"Aren't you involved enough?" Umberto looked shocked at my news, half-appalled at my suggestion.

"Yes, I am. That's not my point, though. I want to help solve this crime. I want to—"

He reached across the table and placed the back of his right hand against my forehead. "You're not feeling well. You have a temperature. The summer flu or something like that has you in its fatal grip, my friend. You should think about keeping away from Zane Ward and abandoning any and all thoughts regarding helping him with this. I strongly suggest you don't become more involved than you already are."

I shook my head and said, "I have to help. I'm in trouble. My ass is on the line. If I don't find myself involved—"

"Don't be a toad, Troy," he pleaded, interrupting. "I want

you alive. You're going to get yourself killed if you help Zane. That man is cute, but reckless and dangerous."

"I have to help. The sooner we end this, the faster we can get back to work and return to our lives. I'm sure you realize how much money we're losing because the salon is closed."

He snapped his fingers four times in a Z shape in midair and exclaimed like a fag, "Girlfriend, I am not helping out! Don't even get that idea into your little queen head! As for the shop being closed...we have no control over that. The law is involved. Keep in mind a murder happened in our building. This isn't going to blow over anytime soon. Patience is needed. That doesn't mean I want to be involved as your sidekick, man."

"I didn't say anything about you helping out with this case."

"I'm just making this clear from the start. I'm a hairdresser and business owner! I'm no Agatha fucking Christie. I don't do murder cases and fight crime!"

I stood up from the table, moved behind him, kissed the top of his Cuban head, and tranquilly said, "Calm down. No one's asking you to be a private dick."

"And they'd better not, if they know what's good for them."

"I get you."

"I'm glad someone does."

"Praise Jesus," I replied, and exited the room.

❖

I was temporarily locked out of my business and apartment, but I still had my dignity, confidence, and cell phone, which wouldn't stop ringing.

The first call was from Mother. "Did you read the paper today?"

"As a matter of fact, I did."

"You've been called a murderer again. This is the second day in a row. I certainly wanted you to achieve fame in your life, but not this way." Her tone was judgmental, which caused me to roll my eyes.

"I've been called worse, Mother. Try growing up queer. Teenage jocks can be atrociously mean. I was called names that would make your stomach turn sour."

"Don't change the subject, Troy Murdock. Tell me you didn't kill that hockey player."

"He played football," I corrected her, and chuckled under my breath. "Of course I didn't kill him."

"Did Umberto? He's black, and black people kill all the time on the news."

"Oh my God, Mother!" I snapped. "Stop being racist! Besides, Umberto is Cuban, not black, and he can't even kill a spider, let alone a professional sports figure."

"The paper said you were lovers with Pieney. Is this true? Are there things you haven't told me?"

I didn't want to go into my personal life with her. "Don't always believe what you read. The newspaper in this corrupt city is slanted."

"Tell me about your Jeep. Did you drown it with gasoline and catch it on fire for insurance money?"

"I didn't do that, Mother. Don't even go there." I tried to stay calm. Mother was a pro at pissing me off, though. I was ready to pull my hair out.

"Who did, then? I'm sure it was one of those hoodlums you hang out with."

I took offense. "Mother, you're so obnoxious sometimes.

I don't know who murdered the football star. But when I find out, you'll be one of the first to hear about it."

"You do love me, don't you?"

I rolled my eyes, shook my head in frustration, and said, "I have always loved you, no matter what the circumstances involve."

"That is so nice to hear, Troy, an obvious reason why I will come and visit you in jail where you'll discover a new boyfriend. I can bring those gingersnaps you like so much."

Did she seriously just say those things? How exasperating. I clarified, "I'm not going to jail."

"You were always my optimistic child, unlike your brother. Cody has never really had the go-get-him style you have."

"Just so you know, I'm innocent. I didn't murder Ben Pieney. Nor did I set my Jeep on fire. I do realize I'm the center of attention regarding the killing, but I didn't have anything to do with it."

"I think that's my other line ringing, honey. Sorry to cut you off, but I have to run."

"Mother!" I screamed into the phone, but the line was already dead, similar to Ben Pieney's current state.

❖

Zane called after Mother. I took the call in the bathroom for privacy, sitting on the closed toilet like a high school girl planning her evening at the prom.

Zane said, "I'll be at the front of the building to pick you up in fifteen minutes. Be ready. I don't have time to wait for you."

"I'm not decent." I looked about the bathroom and

thought, *The decorating is overdone in golds…totally eighties. A remodel is in dire need.*

"Get ready. We have some important business to take care of. I need your help, which means you can't back out on me."

"I'm not prepared to help you yet."

"People tell me lots of things. That doesn't mean I listen to them. Don't make me dress you and toss your ass in my cruiser."

Although it sounded like a great idea and something I wouldn't have minded at all, I said, "I won't help you."

"You don't have an option. I expect you to be ready. And I am not coming up to get you. Be on the street for me."

I rolled my eyes, sighed heavily, and said, "You want me to be your hustler, don't you?"

"Trust me, you can be my hustler any day. I think you already know that."

"You're a fucker, Zane Ward."

"A cute one at that." He hung up on me.

❖

Umberto was at the bathroom door, banging on its plane of smooth wood. He called through the door, "Is everything all right in there? Do you need nine-one-one? What's happening, Troy? Are you dying, darling? You're starting to worry me."

I called out from the toilet, "I'm fine. Thank you for caring."

My phone rang again. That time it was Earl Carbon, my mother's lawyer, sounding like he was suffering from an unnamed plague and coughing into my ear. Carbon cleared his throat and said, "Your mother says you need my help."

"I already have a lawyer. Thank you for soliciting me, though."

"My rates can beat anyone's rates. Besides, we're like family. I can give you twenty percent off your bill."

"I'm not interested."

"Who's representing you? I have a right to know. Tell me. Is it that Margie Hunt woman? Your mother told me she turned you gay. How can you trust a lawyer like that, Troy? How can you—"

I cut Carbon off by saying, "My relationship with Ms. Hunt does not concern you. I'm not in need of your services. Thank you, Earl. And have a nice day." I pressed the Off button.

❖

Just as I was about to exit the bathroom, Umberto and Axel opened the door.

Axel said in his thick, broken English, "We thought you committing murder to yourself."

"Suicide," I corrected him, stepped out of the bathroom, and walked quickly down the hallway toward the Princess Room.

"What's going on, Troy? I need details! I need facts!" Umberto followed me.

Once at the Princess Room, I spun around and said, "Zane is picking me up in about ten minutes. He says we have some business to take care of."

"I don't trust him," Umberto pleaded. "Whatever you decide to do with him, be careful. That man is terribly hot but dangerous."

"I'm sure this will be safe. I'm not his enemy."

"How do you know that? I've watched those cop shows

on TV. Bad cops are out there. The world is full of naughty pigs. You don't know what you're getting yourself into."

"Zane Ward is not a bad cop. Just remember, he's the one keeping the both of us out of jail."

My comment quieted Umberto down.

❖

Zane pulled up to the curb in his green-and-white city cruiser and I climbed inside. I asked, "Are you wearing a new cologne?"

"Kenneth Cole. Do you like it?"

I did. He smelled sexy and freshly showered by a waterfall on a Hawaiian island. "It's sexy as hell."

"I wore it just for you. I'm glad you like it."

"Enough," I said, "let's keep this on a professional level. What kind of business trip is this?"

He mentioned a second visit to Mrs. Pieney, who expected us within the hour. As Zane mumbled about her whereabouts on the night of her youngest son's murder, I discreetly checked him out: clean-shaven with sparkling eyes, pressed khakis, and new shoes. It was obvious he had gone out of his way to impress me with his hygiene. The cop looked new and improved, clean-cut and tasty.

"You can't keep your eyes off me."

"I'm not. You're hallucinating."

"Now you're lying. Just tell me you like what you see and that you want to fuck me, and we can move on with our day."

"I'm admitting nothing." I watched him make a right onto Deffler Street, which would take us to the beltway and the other side of Quill Village where Mrs. Pieney lived at 23 Western Drive.

"I'm sexy and you know it. I have Hollywood looks. I'm a baby doll. Someone you want to fuck around with."

"You're conceited, vain, and an asshole sometimes."

"And sexy as hell. Don't forget that."

I sighed heavily and broke down. "And sexy. There, I said it. Are you happy?"

"Very happy. I knew you wouldn't disappoint me. Thank you for those enlightening compliments. But honestly, I am not as sexy as you."

A smile surfaced at the corners of my mouth, and a warm pang found its way into my stomach.

❖

Mrs. Paula Pieney sat in her kitchen at a high-back chair. A bourbon on the rocks sat in front of her on the table; the semi-filled bottle was positioned to the right of the faux-crystal tumbler. To my surprise, the woman looked nothing like Ben. Fiery-red hair, and black eyes that welcomed our arrival. Paula thrived on our attention/company. Upon our entrance through her back door and into the kitchen, which was wall-to-wall marigold with accents of shocking blue, she cried, "Sit down. Make yourselves comfortable." Then she took a hearty gulp of her before-noon cocktail and glowed with warm niceness.

Both Zane and I decided to stand since there was only one chair available around the table. And following a warm apology with regard to her son's brutal murder, my handsome sidekick asked, "Do you have the names of Ben's friends that can help us out?"

Paula dabbed at tears in her eyes and sniffled. "He didn't have many friends. He was quite reserved and kept to himself, if you want to know the truth."

"Was Blaine Phoenix a friend of Ben's?"

She nodded, poured more bourbon into her tumbler, and replied, "They grew up together. They played football as boys. Blaine was very close to Ben."

Zane asked, "Were they involved...sexually? Did the two share a relationship that was stronger than a friendship?"

Ben's mother shrugged and said, "A mother shouldn't know the details of a son's sex life. I know Ben was different than the other players on his professional team. I realize he enjoyed the company of men, but honestly, I didn't know his boyfriends. He kept that side of his life very private from me, which I respected him for."

"Were there any female friends?" I cut in.

"Ben didn't like girls. He was very fond of young men, particularly handsome ones who were athletic."

"Is there anyone else who can help us to determine your son's murder? Anyone you know that Ben was associated with or very close to who can share some facts with us, besides his Violator teammates and coach?" Zane asked.

She shook her head. "No one that I'm aware of. As I have already said, Ben was a very private man, even with me."

Zane's questioning was over. Before leaving the broken woman to her misery and morning drink, he passed her one of his business cards and said, "If you can think of anyone who can help us find out who did this to your son, Mrs. Pieney, please, let me know."

Ben's mother finished the three fingers of bourbon in her tumbler, nodded, and poured herself another drink.

❖

Back in Zane's cruiser, I said, "She looks like a bulldozer ran over her."

"The woman is shattered and...she needs to grieve."

"If you want to know the truth, I'm surprised she didn't mention Cort."

I didn't know where Zane was taking us. We were back on the beltway and headed south. He zoomed past the Showengale Avenue exit and we ended up on Bossner Street, a local shopping district. Zane turned his head in my direction, crinkled his forehead with uncertainty, and asked, "Who is Cort?"

"Ben's older brother. I thought you knew that."

"I didn't know Ben had an older brother. How do you know about him?"

"Ben mentioned him on our date. The brothers haven't talked in years. Some kind of sibling rivalry or something like that. I guess it was wicked. I gathered they pretty much hated each other."

"What else do you know about the brother?"

"Nothing. That's all Ben told me about him."

Zane replied, "I guess she was too devastated to mention Cort."

"Unless she's hiding something."

He made a right on Wentor Street, shared a gleaming smile with me, and said, "You're going to make a fine partner for me."

"With or without my clothes on?"

"Whatever it takes, pal."

"I doubt that," I said, and wondered what he was going to get us involved in next.

❖

Blaine Phoenix was as big as a brick wall and sexy as hell. We caught him in his white briefs, all groggy-eyed and fresh out of bed. He opened his apartment's front door as he rubbed a fist in his right eye, yawning.

It wasn't a surprise that Phoenix slept the morning and some of the afternoon away. Before arriving at his apartment, Zane briefed me on the guy's background. He worked nights as a straight callboy. Because of his massive size, Phoenix sometimes bounced at straight clubs, just to make some extra cash.

Zane introduced us and asked, "Can we come in?"

I checked Phoenix out from head to toe. The guy stood at six-five and was bear material all the way. He sported hard nipples and mussed black hair. His shoulders were rock solid and his neck was thick with heavy cords. To my surprise, he let us in without questions.

His apartment was untidy and underdecorated, which proved to me that he was straight. An empty pizza box lay open on the coffee table in the living room. Beer bottles were scattered around the room, and a few dirty clothes lay on the floor next to his bed on the opposite side of the room.

"Sorry about the mess. I had a little wake for Ben last night. Have a seat on the couch." Phoenix rushed to the couch and picked up a pair of women's pink panties, a brassiere, and a skirt, all of which he tossed to the floor. He gathered up a few of the beer bottles and carried them into his spacious kitchen. "I really have to piss. I'll be back in a second." He vanished behind a bamboo screen made up of three panels, which almost reached the ceiling.

I made eye contact with Zane. Once he exited his "bathroom area," he went to his kitchen sink and washed his hands.

"You were friends with Ben Pieney, correct?" Zane asked.

Blaine said, "Best friends. We grew up together. We did everything as young boys. Grade school. Junior high. High school. Summer camp. Bible camp. You name it—we were glued at the hip."

"Any animosity between the two of you lately?"

By the confused look on Phoenix's face, I figured he didn't know what "animosity" meant. I asked, "Did you get along well with Ben lately?"

"Most of the time," Phoenix said. He shrugged while he rinsed his hands, and added, "We had a few fights like friends sometimes do."

"Recently?" I inquired.

Phoenix shook his head in a vehement manner. "Not recently."

Zane asked, "Was Ben a client of yours?"

Phoenix chuckled and dried off his hands with a paper towel, which he then tossed in the garbage. "I'm straight. My clients are all female. I didn't have any interest in the man. Besides, Ben had other guys to mess around with."

Zane asked, "You know any of those guys?"

Phoenix shook his head. "Fuck buddies usually don't have names."

I asked, "No way we can find them and talk to them?"

Phoenix picked up a crumpled dark-blue dress shirt from a living room chair. He slipped his arms into the fabric but didn't button it up. "I guess you can ask around at the Diva Club. That was Ben's favorite hangout. I'm sure he found the guys there."

Zane asked, "You know Ben's brother?"

"Yeah. A lot of people know that asshole."

"Why is Cort an asshole?" Zane asked.

"Liar. Thief. You name it and he's it. The guy's a bad egg.

He's into drugs and guns. Ben didn't have any time for that shit."

"Do you know that firsthand?" I asked.

Phoenix shook his head. He found a pair of jeans on his floor, picked them up, stepped into them, one leg at a time, and said, "I don't. You need to know that Cort never did me wrong. We're like brothers, since we grew up together. Close men like us don't fuck each other over. He has his business and I have mine. Neither of us ever crosses that line. I've heard some pretty rough shit about him, though. He's been with the wrong crowd for years and is always in trouble."

"What crowd is that?" Zane asked.

"You know. Druggies. Alcoholics. Mafia guys. Gangsters. Dealers. Cort likes to drink, and that's where he meets his so-called buddies."

"Is he in a gang?" I asked.

Phoenix shook his head and chuckled. "Not Cort. He works alone. Pressure by a gang is not the way he rolls. A gang adds a lot of stress to one's life. Cort is more laid back."

Zane walked over to the bra and panties on the floor, picked up the elegant bra with his right index finger. "Tell me what you were doing on Saturday around three o'clock in the morning."

"What you see is what you get," Phoenix said.

"You make a lot from girls?" my sidekick said.

"I get by. It's comfortable work and pays the bills."

"You make a lot from dudes?" I interjected.

Phoenix shook his head. "I already told you I'm straight. I don't do dick. I'm into holes."

"Never curious about what guys can do together?"

"Never."

"It never hurts to check, right?" Zane finished our

conversation, dropped the bra to the couch, and we said our good-byes.

❖

Zane agreed to drop me off at Umberto's pad. I saw the '88 Buick parked on the street in the shade, half-concealed by a Japanese maple.

"Thanks for helping me out, Troy," he said from behind the steering wheel.

"Sure…because I did a lot."

"Your support was encouraging. I appreciate that, just so you know." He placed his right palm on my left thigh.

"You're flirting with me and you know it." I removed the palm from my thigh and shook my head. "Don't play with me, Zane. I'm not your toy, even if you think I am."

"Is that illegal?"

I patted his shoulder, ignored his question, and climbed out of the cruiser. Before I walked into the apartment building and took the stairs up to Umberto's pad, I said, "I'm just glad you didn't try to murder me this time."

"No problem, sexy guy!" he yelled out his cruiser's open window, and grinned from ear to ear.

CHAPTER SEVEN
BROTHERLY LOVE

U mberto and Axel had left a handwritten note for me on their dining room table. I picked it up and read:

> *Sweetheart—*
> *Went to lunch at Sabio's. Be back after a few*
> *hours of shopping. Our cells are on.*
> *Three Snaps & Kisses,*
> *U/A*

It was a good time to ring my lawyer, Margie Hunt, to discuss the last few days with her. As I began to roll through the name index in my Nextel to find her number, it rang in my hand. The number on my called ID read Unavailable, but I decided to take the call anyway.

"This is Troy."

"You fucking sonofabitch! Who the fuck do you think you are? What do I have to do to get rid of you?" The voice was rough, loud, and obnoxious. It definitely belonged to a woman, someone I had recently pissed off, no doubt.

"Who is this?" I barked into the phone.

"You know who the fuck this is! Don't be a smartass with me!"

I honestly didn't know who it was, but guessed it to be Ivan Reed's lover. "Luanne Ringle?"

"The fuck right it's Luanne Ringle. Listen to me, and listen to me closely. You keep your fucking hands off my man! If I see you with him I'll break every fucking bone in your queer body! Do you fucking hear me?"

"You took Ivan away from me and I should be thanking you for your services. You're a very kind woman to look out for my best interest." I then pressed the Off button on my phone, gathered my nerves, fetched a glass of white wine from a nearby bottle on the kitchen counter, and decided to eat lunch alone at Benders & Slides, two blocks away.

❖

Benders & Slides was a chic little bistro with the cutest waiters. My main eye course was a blond-haired, blue-eyed nineteen-year-old named Dawson, who seemed very nervous around me.

"You're new here, aren't you?" I inquired, feebly flirting with him.

Dawson had pumped biceps and inflated chest, white teeth, perfectly coiffed hair with just the right amount of product, and a narrow waist to cling to. He nodded, smiled, and blushed.

"I'll make this easy for you. One glass of white wine and a spinach-strawberry salad with the mustard-and-onion dressing on the side. Plus, I'll leave you a hearty tip if you keep my wineglass filled at all times. What do you say?"

Dawson clumsily scurried away with my order. I was alone for approximately thirty-two seconds when the chair across from me was pulled out by my handsome older brother, Cody. He sat and said, "You're looking good for all the commotion in your life, little bro."

Cody was a replica of our missing father with cocoa bean–colored hair, yellow-green eyes, astute-looking chin, and extensive shoulders. A journalist for the *Village Caller*, he was thirty this year, and feeling old for maybe the first time in his life. He took a sip of my water, placed the glass back, and said, "Mother is on a tedious rampage about you and this murder thing."

"Mother needs to mind her own business. Talk her into a vacation or something."

"She thinks you killed that quarterback. How are you going to convince her otherwise?" Again, he took a drink of my water and clicked ice cubes against glass.

I loved my brother, but sometimes he irked me. "I don't kill men, I just sometimes fuck them."

My brother merely shared a devilish smile with me and said, "I'm happy to say I'll be taking the heat away from you."

That comment blew me away. Cody usually only cared about himself. Feeling interested in his statement, I asked, "How so?"

Dawson interrupted us. He placed my white wine on the table and shuffled his delightful buttocks away.

My aging brother found the glass of wine, picked it up, took two sips, and returned the wine to the table. "I'm finally introducing Elizabeth to her."

"Elizabeth Bradbaum…the sweet and cheery elementary teacher you're helplessly falling for?"

He nodded and blushed. "Elizabeth wants to meet her. I think tonight is the night. Mother is under a lot of stress because of you and your boyfriend antics. Elizabeth has a very calming presence and can possibly help her."

I sighed heavily and secretly smiled. "Does Elizabeth know Mother is evil toward all boyfriends and girlfriends?"

"I've explained that. She seems brave and enjoys a good challenge."

"Mother is going to eat her up alive and spit her out. There is no way to prepare for her tyrannical behavior."

"I'm aware of that and already briefed Elizabeth. Honestly, I don't exactly know how much help I have offered her, since Mother is a nuclear bomb at times."

"With all due respect, Cody, are you sure this is a good idea?"

"Elizabeth won't have it any other way. It's the next step in our relationship. If I don't do this…I'm quite sure she'll dump me."

For about half a second I felt bad for him. Then I rolled my eyes with the slightest bit of irritation. "It could be your last step. How many nice women have you lost because of our mother?"

"Too many to count. My dating life has always been a shambles because of her shenanigans."

"Exactly. I suggest you not do this." Okay, so I was being nice for a change to my sibling. Elizabeth's introduction to Mother could have easily taken me out of my mother's spotlight. There was one problem, though: I really liked Elizabeth. She was soft, sweet, and rather lovely. She would make a great wife and companion for my brother in the near future. Honestly, I knew Mother could ruin that with one stare; God had it on record that she had accomplished it numerous times before. Elizabeth was salvageable, I thought. A glittery gem. Someone right for my brother. A good sidekick. And a great future sister-in-law for me. "Don't do this. I can handle Mother's rage about the quarterback and his unexpected murder. Run away with Elizabeth and move to Spain. Get married. Have a bunch of kids. Save her and yourself while you can."

Cody shook his head. "Dinner's at eight."

"I can't make it."

"You have to make it."

"I can't witness Elizabeth's destruction. She is your diamond in the rough."

Cody rolled his eyes and said, "You're being a drama queen."

"This dinner will be your broken heart after it's all over with."

"I doubt that, little bro," he said, took another sip of my white wine, and then left.

I was then left alone with my good-looking waiter, and some heavy-duty flirting.

❖

I did attend dinner with Mother, Cody, and Elizabeth.

The woman was not your typical mother. She wanted her two city boys to live under her roof for the rest of our lives so she could take care of us. Mother wanted to keep us young forever. She hated our friends, lovers, and careers. She wanted me to be a taxi driver so I could take her wherever she needed to go. Cody was supposed to be a mailman because she always needed to get her mail: coupons, flyers, Hallmark cards, and gift certificates from friends. Truth was, Mother's disappointment in her two boys ran pretty deep. And it was quite irritating to know that she liked Cody's girlfriends and my boyfriends more than she liked us.

Minnie loathed Elizabeth Bradbaum, even though the elementary teacher was petite, soft-spoken, and very mannerly. Even as she shook hands with the woman, took her purse and jacket, she seethed that Elizabeth came to dinner. Displeased, she said, "So, this is the woman who is corrupting my boy."

"Mother!" I snapped. "Be nice!"

Cody looked stunned, open-mouthed and pale.

Liz acted like the comment never happened and complimented Mother's house. "It's so comfortable and appealing. Did you decorate it yourself?"

Mother ignored her, kissed Cody's forehead, and told us to be seated in the dining room, as dinner was ready.

Cody and his girlfriend were seated at the dining room table. I decided to give the two a few minutes alone and chatted with Mother in the kitchen.

Mother immediately closed in on me and said, "She's a cat. Look at those eyes. That woman is sneaky."

"I'm sure she doesn't shit in a sandbox, though."

Mother scolded, "Don't be rude."

"You're overreacting. Liz—as she wants to go by, so don't call her Beth or Betty, Mother—is a dove. She's very good for Cody. Besides, your son is falling in love with her and you have to respect that. That woman is going to give you grandbabies in the near future."

"My son should have been a mailman. Look what he's doing with his life. And that woman will not provide me with grandbabies—she's going to birth a litter of cats."

I rolled my eyes, handed her a platter of roast pork loin with a side of applesauce, and said, "Go back in there and be nice. Make Cody proud of you."

Frankly, dinner was a disaster. Over the pork loin, Mother told Betsy—as she called her—that she had a big bottom and a low IQ, and dressed like an old librarian.

Cody was appalled and roared, "You're being discourteous! How can you say those things to her? You don't even know Liz."

Mother called Cody a Neanderthal, just like our father, and…

Liz Bradbaum bolted from the house, crying. All of us heard the front door open and slam closed.

I followed behind her in distress, but she was fast and had already climbed into her Smart car and putted away.

To my surprise, Zane Ward pulled into Mother's drive in his green-and-white cruiser and met me on the sidewalk leading to the circus inside. Behind me, Mother and Cody were screaming at each other about Liz being a feline critter.

Zane was a breath of fresh air to see and smell. His chiseled smile lit up my evening for a moment and caused me to feel warm and fuzzy inside. He smelled like ash soap with just a hint of perspiration. He walked up to me and said, "You look devastated, Troy. What's going on?" Anger between mother and brother inside the Tudor-style house drew Zane's attention away from me for a second. He said, "I hear what's going on."

"Can we get out of here?" I asked, practically begging him.

"You're reading my mind. That's why I'm here. I need your help again."

"What kind of help?"

"Get in the cruiser and I'll tell you on the way."

I obliged, happy to leave dinner, Mother, and my brother behind. I was blessed that Zane came to my rescue, for maybe the first time since I met him.

❖

A minute later we were seated in his cruiser and already two blocks from Minnie's house. My sidekick said, "Here, take this. You might need it." He reached under his driver's seat, pulled out a Taser stun gun, and passed it to me.

"Where are we going and what do I need this for?" I

delicately took the gun from him and checked it out: palm-size for compact carrying and use, rubberized coating for a good grip, safety switch, and a wrist strap.

"Be careful with it. You don't want to stun yourself."

I said, "Dinner with Mother, Cody, and his new girlfriend has already left me stunned. Trust me when I say that this thing is like a toy for me."

"Thattaboy, Troy." Zane laughed.

"So tell me, where are you taking me?"

"Sit back, enjoy the ride, and listen to me…"

❖

The gay club Underground Pink on Canasta Street was owned by Cort Pieney, Ben's brother. Zane had a few questions to ask the guy. He wanted my company, which was why he found me at Mother's. Maybe he needed protection, too, which was probably why I was sporting the stun gun.

As we pulled up to the club, which was located beneath a launderette, I asked, "Is this a date?"

Zane turned his cruiser off and shifted his attention in my direction. "Do you want it to be a date?"

"I was thinking dinner and a movie would be a nice date. A walk, too. Some dancing. A coffee with a French dessert. This isn't a date. This is more like an errand together."

"You're exactly right. This is not a date, Troy."

We walked down twenty cement steps and entered Underground Pink, which was creepy and dark, smelled of urine and semen, and thumped with wall-trembling music by Korn. The place was empty at the moment, except for a few alcoholics in chains at the bar. I followed adorable Zane up to the U-shaped bar and listened to him ask the hairless bartender if we could speak to Cort.

"He's not here," the bartender said, wiping off the bar with a wet towel.

Zane pulled out his Quill Village Police Department badge and asked, "Is he here now?"

He nodded. "He's in the back. Let me tell him he has company."

Approximately two minutes later we were escorted into a rear room with a small desk and two chairs. The walls were black and a heavy pot smell hung in the air.

A blond woman who looked like Marilyn Monroe buttoned up a cotton shirt. She left Cort's office and closed the door after her exit.

Cort Pieney was seated behind his desk. He was bare-chested and his pants were unbuttoned. He was nicely built, like his murdered brother. It was quite clear to me he was pissed about our untimely intrusion. He didn't smile like Ben and seemed less concerned with his hygiene, as evidenced by the scruff on his cheeks and his strong body odor. Angrily, he asked, "What the fuck do you two want?"

Zane flashed his badge and told the brother his name and position. He said, "I have a few questions for you about Ben's murder."

Cort immediately said, "I don't know anything about that. Ben had his life and I have mine."

Zane stood solid beside me, brave and alert, and asked, "You weren't close to your brother?"

"Never. He was the good son and…I have this." Cort lifted his right arm and presented his foul-smelling office.

"Did anyone have something against your brother?"

"I don't know. Ben and I never talked. He played football and I run a bar."

"He didn't visit you here?"

"Never." Cort shook his head.

"And you can't help me?"

"No."

"You don't want to find out who killed Ben?"

The brother shook his head, cold and alert. "I didn't even know the guy. After high school, he went his way and I went mine. We liked it that way. He enjoyed guys and I enjoyed girls. It's been like that every since."

"You know a Blaine Phoenix?" Zane asked.

I gripped the Taser in my front pocket. It wasn't a real gun, but part of me wanted it to be. Cort looked like a mobster: shady, dangerous, and rugged. There was no doubt in my mind that he had an arrangement of weapons in the desk where he sat, perhaps ready to blast us away at any moment.

Cort shook his head and replied, "Never heard of the guy."

"You know any guys from the Violators that Ben hung out with?"

"None, pal. You're asking the wrong person these questions. Go waste someone else's fucking time. I got a business to run. I have things to do."

Our visit was over. Cort Pieney wasn't about to help us and Zane knew it. On our way out of the bar, the bartender growled at me. I kept up my pace, nervous as hell, and felt out of my realm, misplaced.

❖

Zane drove me back to my mother's house on Wilde Street. I didn't go inside to console her about the disastrous dinner with Cody's girlfriend. Instead, I climbed into the '88 Buick, drove back to Umberto's apartment, and found myself locked out.

I called Umberto's cell, but it was turned off; Axel's was

too. I thought about spending the night at the local Holiday Inn, but hotel rooms were not comfortable. What was I to do? I thought about it for the next few minutes, sucked up a little bit of pride and courage, dialed Zane's cell, and politely said, "You'll never guess what happened to me."

"You figured out who's Ben Pieney's murderer?"

"I'm locked out of Umberto's apartment and need a place to sleep."

"My bed is always available to you, Troy."

"I was thinking about your couch."

"The bed is more comfortable."

"The couch is more safe."

"Have it your way. I'll leave the kitchen door open for you. Just don't get mad if I end up hitting on you."

❖

I arrived at Zane's house on Broad Street approximately ten minutes later. He was conveniently freshly showered and sported a white towel around his narrow waist. Droplets of shower water sparkled all over his rugged-looking chest as he stood at the kitchen counter and poured himself a cup of decaf coffee. He asked, "Would you like a taste?"

"The coffee or you?" I asked, and believed it a bad idea to spend the night. Maybe the Holiday Inn wasn't such a lousy place to stay after all.

"Both. You can have a cup of coffee now…and then me, later."

"I'm not here for sex."

He passed me the cup of steamy coffee, which I accepted. He then began to pour his own cup and said, "I'm not free. If you sleep with me, there's always a payment. You know that, I'm sure."

"I have credit with you since you almost tried to kill me. If I want to fuck you tonight, I won't have to pay a damn cent," I flirted, and felt warmed and soothed by the coffee.

"In fact, if you decide to taste me, the payment's pretty high."

"Unfortunately, Zane, I won't be tasting you this evening."

He faced me. "That's a terrible shame. I'm in a very edible mood. Something tells me I'm a pretty sweet guy. What do you think?"

"I'm no longer into bald, sexy guys." I took in his beautiful face and eyes and tried not to study his sculpted chest.

"That's a terrible shame. Because a bald, sexy guy likes you." Zane approached my lips with his.

I blocked the kiss with my marigold coffee mug and took a sip. Then I said, "Is this our beer and pizza date that we agreed to?"

"Do you want it to be?"

"I haven't made up my mind yet."

"You're not interested in me?"

"I don't want to take advantage of you."

"If you really wanted to, my skin is yours."

"But I won't. I don't play that game."

"I understand. I'm a little disappointed, but I completely understand."

An hour later, I was alone in his spare room on the second floor, next to the bathroom. Zane wanted to tuck me in for the night, which I passed on. He said, "Good night, John Boy," on the other side of the door.

I replied, "Good night," in the dark, under a sheet and comforter, and drifted contentedly into sweet dreams.

Chapter Eight
Sexy Ass

A round three o'clock in the morning I woke up in Zane's bed, naked and in his arms. I felt his firm erection against my bottom, his breath on the back of my neck, and his torso against my back. Slowly, I pulled away from him, ready to search out my own room.

Zane was awake and whispered, "You just got here, where are you going?"

"I've been sleepwalking again, haven't I?"

"It's not a bad thing. I was just getting comfortable with you. Spend the rest of the night with me."

I turned over and faced him. Early-morning moonlight shifted in through the window behind me and appeared in his amber-colored eyes. I admired his rigid face and perfect smile. My eyes traveled down and over the shadow of his plated torso, firm nipples, and rippled stomach.

"Stay with me. I won't hurt you," he pleaded.

"What if I want you to hurt me?" I teased. My hand found the smoothness of his taut navel, bristly patch of pubic hair, and the stiff erection between his legs. I touched the cock's head with two fingers, leaned in for a kiss, and turned naughty within a matter of seconds.

Following some heavy petting and chest licking, Zane said, "I want to suck you, Troy."

I couldn't respond. My head was elsewhere, confused, lost and dizzy. I felt him roll me onto my back. He gently climbed between my legs and began to lick me, causing me to moan. I held his head against me with my right hand.

Zane was a master and continued his adventure for the next fifteen minutes.

"I'm going to make you spew tonight, guy. We're just getting started now." He found my pert nipples with his tongue, then both armpits, puckered navel, and my plump cock again, then my balls, and...

"Jesus, what's going on down there, Zane?"

He had my legs up and spread apart, and his lips nuzzled against my pink and hairless opening. The detective lapped at my tight hole, seemingly overcome with a sexual buzz from his pleasure. His fingers found my nipples, which he twisted and squeezed in a gentle manner. His tongue roved over my skin and his plump lips dabbed kisses to my inner thighs, scrotum, and back to my tight core.

Eventually, he pulled off for air and said between my legs, "You're driving me crazy...I really want to fuck you." He climbed off the bed and fetched a condom and lube from one of his drawers.

Seconds later, I had my heels on his shoulders and the head of his plastic-covered shaft pushed into my bottom—three inches...five inches...six inches—until all of his rod was inside me. I was breathless and light-headed beneath him. The detective gently flicked my nipples with his fingertips and grunted and groaned above me. He moved wildly inside me, pulled out, and pushed in again.

Windblown, intoxicated by his lust, and swept away in

a foggy hallucination, I felt a vibration skirt its way through my body. My toes and spine quivered. Every pore on my flesh opened and allowed his lust to permeate there. The euphoria between us was heightened to an unstoppable level. Soon I would explode…burst…erupt with deep satisfaction.

Together we built a sweet sweat as our rhythm rose in a perfect crescendo. He banged my bottom for over fifteen minutes until he couldn't take it anymore, ready to burst. He pulled out of me, ripped the condom from his rod, and dropped it to the floor. In a matter of seconds, he said, "We'll come together," and placed his cock against mine, joining the two with his soft hand. He worked the cocks in harmonized motion, stroke after stroke. Together we mumbled like youthful boys, releasing our creamy loads onto my chest, and sprayed the sticky sap against my ripped torso, peaklike nipples, and rounded chin.

❖

Spent, I lay in his arms, cuddled against his naked skin. Again, Zane breathed on my neck, happy to be with me, ready to fall asleep.

"Zane?" I whispered.

"I'm here," he murmured groggily.

"He's still out there."

"Who's still out there?"

"The person who killed Ben."

"Shhh. Forget about it. You're safe in my arms," he said in a hollow tone and squeezed me against his naked body, exactly where I wanted to be.

❖

I've never had breakfast in bed after spending the night with a lover. People tell me it's a wonderful thing to wake up to. Truthfully, I was blown away when Zane walked into his bedroom with no shirt on carrying a tray filled with orange juice, wheat toast, one egg, and a single orchid.

I sat up and asked, "Where did you get the orchid?"

He placed the tray on the bed and sat next to me. He kissed my cheek. "You really want to know?"

"I do." I tried a corner of toast in some dippy egg and found it delicious.

"My neighbor has a lovely garden. I stole it when no one was looking."

I laughed, feeding him a bite of toast.

He chewed it up and swallowed. "We've got big plans today."

"Such as?"

"Ben hung around two guys on his football team. Jonas Smith and Davido Cheswick. The Violators have practice at Torton Field and we're going to pay them a visit."

"I have to eat and shower first."

"And do something else, maybe," he greedily suggested, pushed his right hand under the sheet, and investigated the goods between my legs.

"By the way," I said, "what happened between us last night?"

"A fairy godfather told me you needed a detective's cock."

"He's a very smart fairy."

"And you're a very sexy one," he said, dotted a kiss to my forehead, and squeezed the tool between my legs.

"You're naughty."

"For all the right reasons, of course."

❖

Torton Field was south of the city, next to the Ipswich River. Zane was behind the wheel of his police cruiser, which meant we could park anywhere we wanted. Thank God, he was a gentleman and didn't take a handicapped spot. The day was sunny and bright with just a few puffy white clouds in the sky. Once the cruiser was parked, we walked into Torton Field and passed a sign that read *Players' Entrance*.

I was a little surprised to find out that Zane knew and liked football. He rattled off a few names, stats, and players' numbers. I followed him down a ramp to Level One, then down a second ramp, and found myself in the stands at the fifty yard line.

Bulky players of different ethnic groups battled it out on the field. Coach Luke Bassett had half of the Violators in shirts and the other half played as skins. I whispered to Zane in a mischievous manner, "I'm rooting for the skins."

He chuckled and agreed with me.

For the next twenty minutes or so the hulking team carried out a few plays. I studied number 59 and enjoyed the powerful span of his shoulders. Zane pointed out number 17, a fullback with lats to die for; he was the guy we were looking for, Jonas Smith. He also pointed out number 35, Davido Cheswick, a tight end who, in my opinion, lived up to his position. Together we watched the professional players execute practice. Bodies flew around the field like beanbags. The football zoomed through the sky from the fifty yard line to one of the goalposts a number of times. Numerous goals were scored by the skins. And after an hour, Coach Bassett blew his whistle and screamed something we couldn't hear.

But seconds later, the team exited the field and headed toward the locker room and showers.

Zane and I walked back up the two ramps and entered Level One. I followed him through a door marked *Private*, down two flights of steel steps, and through a second door. To my astonishment and delight I read the eight-by-six red-and-white sign on the wall: VIOLATORS' LOCKER ROOM.

Vinnie Castanetti was positioned at the door. The guy looked like he ate humans for lunch: big and sweaty, grim-faced with a bad complexion, and two times the size of a Volkswagen. Vinnie and Zane grew up in Quill Village and played football together as kids. The two men shook hands

Vinnie honored us with a smile and said, "How you doin', Zane?" with a Brooklynesque accent that I found a bit awkwardly sexy.

"Fine, Vinnie. How's your better half doing?"

"Better than usual. Enjoying summer. The two of us are going to the Grand Canyon next month. Nick's been dying to get away."

"A good place to go. You'll have a fine time there."

Vinnie didn't ask to see Zane's credentials. He unlocked the door with a silver key around his neck and said, "Go right in…The guys are starting to take their showers now. Make yourselves comfortable."

My detective sidekick escorted me down a narrow hallway with dim lights. I heard masculine chatter and showers spraying water. The hallway sloped upward, made a left, and welcomed the two of us into the Violators' locker room.

❖

If there was a place called heaven, I believed it to be inside our home team's locker room. I saw Otter Conrad's immense and dark chest, number 82's compact ass, the kicker's naked thighs, and Reed Thompson's seven inches between his muscled legs.

Zane politely whispered into my ear, "Close your mouth. Don't make a scene. Not everyone on the team is queer. You don't want to get the shit kicked out of you, so listen to me."

I listened to him and shut my trap. To look more like an investigator, I studied the locker room: benches to the left, right, and middle; red lockers to the left and white lockers to the right; a shower area beyond the lockers, to the rear of the room. I admired a darling twenty-one-year-old towel boy, three physical fitness trainers, a handsome doctor, and Bassett, who just happened to look like a bulldog.

Zane found Jonas Smith by his locker, dressing after a shower. The skyscraper with olive-colored skin and amethyst-colored eyes, long black hair, and a scar that lined his upper lip was affable with Zane and me.

The detective beside me cut to the chase and passed on formalities. He asked Jonas, "Were you pals with Ben Pieney?"

"We're all pals around here. There's no 'I' in team."

"You spend some quality time off the field with Ben?"

"Are you asking if we sucked each other's cocks? Because if that's what you are asking, padre, it's none of your business." Jonas slipped into a pair of wrinkle-free khakis and a white T-shirt the size of a bedspread. "I don't want to be rude," Jonas continued, "but I'm not the kind of guy to spread around who I get in the sack with."

"I'm simply asking if the two of you hung out together. Were you friends as well as teammates? Did you do anything together outside of your games? Did you have beer on Sundays when you weren't playing? Did you—"

"I get it. Let's just say I had Pie's back. That's what we

called him around here. He liked that name. I was his friend. Someone who cared about him. And if I catch the son of a bitch who sliced his throat, I'll do the same thing to him."

"So you're saying you have some remorse for Ben?" Zane sounded serious, half on edge, and rather sure-minded.

"I'd be an animal if I didn't. Pie was a big part of this team, and now he's not. That's a huge adjustment. That's a lot of grief and remorse. This team has a lot of growing to do. Somehow we have to figure out how to do that without Pie's help." Jonas slipped on a short-sleeved cashmere shirt that was baby blue, and continued, "Pie was a good guy. Everyone on this team believed that. He was honest and humble. He never let the fucking game get to his head. He never complained about all the little shit. Pie was just decent, the all-American quarterback everyone falls in love with."

"And how much did you know about him off the field?"

"He was the same kind of guy off the field as he was on. We played poker together on a few nights. We went to the movies once. We went drinking on a few occasions."

"Did Ben have an alcohol problem?"

"You can't make the championships as the nation's number one quarterback and be an alcoholic. Life doesn't work that way."

"You know of any enemies he might have had?"

"Absolutely not. He loved too many people. These guys. His mother. Just about everybody. Pie was too nice a guy to have his neck sliced open. Whoever murdered him needs to burn in hell."

Zane asked, "What were you doing at approximately three o'clock in the morning on July tenth?"

"The time Pie got sliced?"

Zane nodded. "That's right. Where were you? What were you doing?"

"Sleeping. In a bed."

"Were you alone?"

"That's none of your business."

"Of course it's my business. And it's Ben's mother's business. If you don't tell me where you were and who you were with, I can cuff you right here and now and embarrass the fuck out of you in front of your peers. What do you think of that?"

I was impressed. My sidekick was not at all intimidated by the fullback's size, nor all of his teammates. He was there to do his job and get it done.

"I was out of town," Jonas said. "I was visiting a friend in Cleveland."

"What friend?"

"Another football player."

"Who?" Zane asked, seriously calm.

"I don't want to say. The last thing I want to happen is the exposure of my personal life."

Zane shook his head. "That isn't going to happen. Trust me. Tell me who you were with."

Jonas paused, stared deeply into Zane's eyes, and seemed to analyze the man from inside out. Eventually, he said, "Timmy Henner from the Cleveland Cougars."

"Another quarterback, right?"

"I'm partial to quarterbacks. What can I say?"

"I guess you are," Zane said. "Where'd you stay?"

Jonas leaned forward, face-to-face with Zane, and whispered, "In his bed. I can prove it. We see each other on the weekends when we're not working on the field."

"You sleep with Ben Pieney, too?"

Jonas shook his head and said, "Never. We were strictly friends."

Coach Bassett broke up our threesome. He bolted toward

us and shouted in his bulldog manner, "What the fuck's going on over here?"

Zane flashed his shield. "I was just asking Jonas a few questions."

"Not in here you won't. Not during my time with these guys." Bassett shook his head and escorted us to a quick exit, back to Vinnie Castanetti's side. Once we were out of the locker room, Bassett snapped at Vinnie, "Keep a close eye on these jokers! I don't want them in my locker room fucking around again! And make sure you do your job or someone else will be doing it for you!"

Vinnie understood.

Zane understood.

I understood.

❖

We returned to Zane's cruiser in the parking lot and waited for Davido Cheswick to exit Torton Field. The cruiser was hidden between a Dumpster and a Durango, which gave us just enough space to be able to see when the tight end exited the locker room and climbed into his Jaguar on the west side of the building. Zane used the speakerphone on his cellular and called the station. He asked, "Did you dig up anything on the pin lodged in Pieney's throat?"

"I've checked all thirty-seven companies in the tri-state area that make pins like the one found in Ben's throat. Not a single one of those companies have any record of creating the slogan on Pieney's pin."

"You're going to have to go broader. Someone's responsible for producing that pin. If you have to go to China, do it." Zane sounded curt and to the point.

"I'm on it, boss. As soon as I find something out, you'll be the first to know."

Zane asked, "What about Blaine Phoenix? Did you talk to him?"

"I did, and got nothing on him. His alibi is strong and true. Can't touch him. He was with a client, Mrs. Olivia Bain from New Hampton. She's seen Phoenix twice a week for the past year. Blames it on a bad marriage. A middle-aged man who doesn't pay attention to her. Another story. Another time. I also checked out Umberto Clemente, his lover Axel Bartholm, and all of Umberto's employees at the salon. They are all solid with alibis. No one raises a flag of interest."

I was happy Umberto, his lover, and my staff at the shop were in the clear. The last thing I wanted to deal with was to learn that one or more was a suspect.

"Anything else?" Zane asked.

The officer's voice echoed inside the cruiser: "You got a pencil or pen? You might want to jot these names down and check these two guys out."

"Who?" Zane reached between the seats for a small notepad and writing implement.

"I think I found Pie's fuck buddies."

"How'd you do that?"

"When I visited Phoenix at his apartment, he left his address book out on a desk and I took a quick look inside, searching for Pie's name. The quarterback's numbers and address were in the book. And next to Pie's name were two other names, which I assumed were more than just friends to Phoenix, if you know what I mean. I'm thinking Pieney shared the guys with Phoenix."

"You're saying those other men listed were his fuck buddies?" Zane asked.

"Can't prove it just yet, but I have a strong vibe that might suggest it."

"Nice work. What are the names?"

"Jonas Smith and Davido Cheswick." Nina spelled out the names for Zane.

"What makes you think they were fuck buddies?" Zane asked.

"Above the names he had two initials, F and B. They could mean football...frank and beans...or guys he liked to fuck around with. I'm going with the latter guess, of course."

"Again, nice work."

"I'm on my way to question Cort Pieney right now. I'll check in with you afterward, boss."

❖

I asked Zane, "You think Jonas Smith was lying to us about sleeping with Ben?"

"Something tells me he was," he said, and peered out the windshield.

"You think Phoenix has Jonas down as a client in his address book?"

"Maybe. We'll have to check into that."

"Even if Phoenix said he was straight and didn't fuck guys?"

"I'm straight," he said. "I only fuck girls."

"That's a lie and you know it," I replied, and poked his shoulder with my right index finger.

Zane looked over at me. He patted my left thigh with his right palm and said, "My point exactly. Phoenix is lying."

Two minutes later, we saw Davido Cheswick exit Torton Field and walk across the parking lot. He was in his early twenties with blond curly hair, brown eyes, and a muscular build. Not a daddy. Not a twink. Somewhere between the two. The guy was handsome and could have passed for a model. His hair was cut short and he was dressed in a pair of tight jeans, a chest-clinging T-shirt, and leather loafers.

He said, "That's our guy right there."

"The one climbing into the silver Jaguar?"

"That's him."

"We going to follow him?"

"You bet your sexy ass, Troy."

And so we did.

CHAPTER NINE
THE VILLAGE OF BATH

We followed Davido Cheswick's silver Jaguar through the city. The sporty car made a right onto Market Street. We watched him park his expensive, bullet-shaped vehicle in a private lot. Three minutes later we observed Davido as he exited the private lot. He made a left on Market and entered one of Quill Village's last operating bathhouses, called the Village of Bath.

Some ugly events had happened at the Village of Bath in the past ten years that had caused it to gain a bad rap. The place was known for drug dealers who carried out their business in the small rooms and pedophiles who took their underage boys there to rape them. Other nontraditional dealings occurred behind the steel door: male hustlers at work, two murders, numerous abductions, and three suicides. In truth, I was surprised the place was still in operation.

Zane opened the steel door and walked into a foyer made up of cement blocks, no windows, and a second steel door. The only thing visible inside the room was an obese man in his mid-forties who sat behind a card table; the second steel door was directly behind him.

"Happy Larson," Zane said, smiled broadly, and nodded in a pleasant manner.

"What the fuck are you doing here? And what the fuck do you want?" Happy asked, unhappily.

Happy Larson was Robert Larson's younger brother. Both men were sex addicts who owned and operated the Village of Bath, two porn shops, and a drug ring, and enjoyed the company of underage blond boys with electrifying blue eyes and thick London accents. Happy was well-to-do and could quit what he was doing to help out his older brother. Unfortunately, Happy was passionate on the subject of his unlawful duties as a crooked Quill Village businessman, and about his sibling. In truth, Happy owned a beautiful mansion in Miami, where a lovely wife named Beatrice Rose Larson didn't know what her hubby did for fun with little blond boys.

Zane handled our entrance into the bathhouse, since Happy wasn't too keen about our arrival. "A detective has needs." He pulled me to his side and ran his tongue along my neck.

The lick caused a shiver of excitement to race through my center.

"I have a weakness for blonds," Happy said. "That's a nice piece of blond there...if you know what I mean."

Zane nodded and gently pulled away from me. Before I knew it, my trusted companion twirled me around and showed off my ass. He spanked it twice with his right palm and asked, "Now tell me, Happy, isn't this the kind of ass you would like to fuck?"

"Sure as hell. That's my kind of ass. Are you selling him to me?"

I was pleased that Zane shook his head. "I'm afraid not, my friend. I want him all for myself. But when I'm done with him, you can have him."

Happy laughed in a hearty manner, head back and neck jiggling.

"Now you know why I'm here," Zane said.

I turned around and Zane lifted my T-shirt. As Happy drooled with hunger, my detective friend informed him, "He needs to be fucked, and the Village is where I want to get the job done."

"I'm flattered, Detective Ward. Honestly, I didn't think you had it in you."

Zane dropped my T-shirt and covered my torso. He pulled out his wallet and paid Happy a hundred bucks for our entrance. Happy took the money, slipped it into his front pocket, found a bronze-colored key in the same pocket, and unlocked the second steel door, letting us inside.

Behind me, Happy said, "Don't forget about giving me that man's ass when you're done with it...I'd be glad to have him as my pet."

Zane answered with a convincing grin. "I'll think about it. You'll be the first on my list to own him."

The second steel door closed and bolted behind us. We were locked in a dim blue hallway with ten doorless rooms. Steam wafted out of the communal rooms and into the hallway as guttural and masculine grunts and groans filled our ears.

I leaned into Zane and asked, "Is this now considered a date for us?"

He enfolded my torso in his arms. He shook his head and whispered, "Not quite. I'll keep you posted, though." The man then kissed me on my right cheek, pulled away, and added, "I'm sorry about showing you off to Happy. I didn't know how else we were going to get in here if I didn't."

"No problem. Secretly, I've always wanted to be treated like a whore. Now I can check that off my bucket list."

"You're not a whore. Don't ever say that about yourself. The Troy Murdock I know is a gentleman through and through, and should be respected. I humiliated you in front of Happy and treated you like a piece of meat. That's my bad and I'm sorry." Zane sounded sincere, although there was a smirk of mischievousness hidden at the corners of his mouth that I simply found attractive.

I was light-headed against him, moved by his words. "Trust me, if that's the worst thing that happens to me on a date with you, I don't have anything to worry about."

"Let me remind you that we're not on a date." He kissed me again. The kiss was smooth and rough at the same time, exactly what I preferred. His five o'clock shadow brushed against my cheeks. His tongue explored my mouth with spontaneous bliss. Once he pulled away from me and wiped the back of his left hand across his mouth, he continued, "You're merely helping me with the case. Take it for what it's worth."

"And you're protecting me."

"Exactly, Troy. Now you're getting it."

❖

Zane pulled me into the first room on our left, which was wall-to-wall lockers and smelled like the back room of a hustler club. Two tables were filled with folded white towels for our use. On each table was an aluminum bowl with complimentary condoms and travel-size tubes of lube. He told me to strip down and snag a towel for my sexy bod. He grabbed a condom and some lube.

"I thought we were just coming to find Davido Cheswick?"

He was already out of his shoes and dress shirt, which he piled at his feet. He shrugged his shoulders, winked at me, and informed me in a hushed tone, "It will be more convincing if we look the part. We'll catch him off guard. And who knows...I just might want to bang you in here."

My stare settled on his beefy chest. Zane slipped off his white briefs and socks.

He caught my up-down stare and asked, "What are you looking at?"

I began to undress, jeans and Texas-size buckle, flats kicked off, cotton Aussiebums exposed. "You sure we're not on a date?"

"Hand me a towel before I use this on you," he teased, cupping his soft rod and balls in his right hand.

I grabbed a towel from the pile and tossed it his way. The cop caught it, slipped it around his waist, and crammed his detective attire into one of the small lockers attached to the wall. He removed the silver key from the locker's door and placed it inside a miniscule pocket on his cotton towel, turned to me, and asked, "Are you ready to get sleazy?"

"Ready as I'll ever be, pal."

"You ever been in a place like this?" Zane asked.

I shook my head. "How about you?"

"Once. A few years back. Let's just say it was one of the worst dates of my life."

I pulled off my navy boxer-briefs and noticed that my sidekick was checking me out.

"You look good, Troy. Nice ass. Nice chest. You and I may have to have a date here after all."

I kicked off my boxer-briefs, folded my clothes nicely, placed everything into a locker next to his, and removed the key from its door.

When I spun around, Detective Ward stood there with a towel ready for me and said, "Too bad you have to use this. I like what I see." After he handed over the towel, he pushed his bare chest against my bare chest. Discreetly, the tips of our noses rubbed together, as well as our upper lips.

"Although I'm captivated by you, I think we should keep this professional until after hours," I suggested, pulling away from him.

"Are you playing hard to get?" he teased.

"Call it what you want." I released myself from his firm grip and walked out of the room and into the dim hallway of warm steam.

❖

Davido Cheswick was in the third room on the right side of the hallway. Some black-haired Asian American dude around twenty years old was on his knees and nestled between Davido's pumped legs. Davido craned his neck and let out a gasp of excitement. He had his palms on the back of his lover's skull.

Davido spotted us in the doorway. Zane was still in role-playing mode and removed his towel. He showed off his goods.

I didn't do the same thing, unsure of what might transpire in the room with four dudes. Never had I experienced a foursome/orgy before. Besides, Zane and I were at the bathhouse on business, not to get laid. There was no reason to get off track. Instead, business was business and we needed to find out what type of relationship Davido had with Pieney.

The room was pretty basic, I noticed. Davido sat on a stainless steel bed against the battleship-gray cement wall opposite the door. To the right of the bed was a stainless steel sink with running water for post-sex cleanup; a stack of fresh towels that smelled like lavender sat to the right of the sink. Beneath the sink was an aluminum basket for dirty towels. To the left of the bed were three marble steps that led down to a standard in-ground bath. The water was illuminated with an aquamarine light at the bottom. Another aquamarine light hung on the wall over Davido's head and flooded the room in muted blue-green.

Zane walked up to the Violator's left side in a seductive manner. He allowed Davido to lick his chest around his right nipple. Zane propped his right leg onto the stainless steel bed to showcase his goods. Balls and dick swung in Davido's face, inches from his lips. Zane asked, "Do you want to fuck me?"

Davido removed one of his palms from his Asian boy's skull and cupped Ward's goods. Davido nodded, delighted with the idea. Just as he was about to move his tongue down into Zane's private area, Zane quickly backed off and said, "I don't think so. That's not the reason why I'm here."

Davido knew something was up and pushed the Asian American boy away from his crotch. A look of startled concern crossed over the young man's handsome face. Davido snatched up his white cotton towel, covered his erection, and asked, "What the fuck's going on here?"

Zane was already in his towel. He stood in the center of the room.

The Asian American boy rose from his knees, found a cotton towel of his own, and bolted past me.

A panicked look settled over Davido's face. His eyes grew wide and his mouth was partially open. He asked again, "What the fuck's going on here?"

Zane was a professional and took his time. Just as Davido was about to stand and bolt out of the room, Zane walked up to him and pushed his palm into the athlete's right shoulder, which forced Davido to sit back down.

"Buddy," Davido said, "I'm not looking for trouble. I just want to shoot my load and leave."

Zane chuckled arrogantly and said, "I'm Detective Zane Ward and I have a few questions for you."

Davido asked, "You're Quill Village's Man of the Year last year, right?"

My partner nodded and presented a pretty-boy smile in a cocky and sexy manner. "That's me."

The football player stuck out his right hand for a shake.

Zane didn't want to shake hands. Instead he asked, "What do you know about Ben Pieney's death?"

The suspect withdrew his hand and placed it back on the cotton towel that covered his middle. He pointed at me and asked, "Who's the other guy?"

"My assistant...Troy Murdock."

"The same guy who got his Jeep blazed?" Davido asked in alarm. Fear skirted across his eyes.

News found its way around the Village, and fast. Zane nodded and questioned, "What do you know about Pieney?"

"Not a lot." Davido shrugged. Both nicely built pecs flexed.

"I don't believe that."

Davido was intimidated by my cohort's interrogation tactics for some reason. Maybe it was because he was naked. "What do you want to know?"

"How long did you know Ben?" Zane said.

"Two years. Why?"

"Were you two buddies outside of playing football?"

"Sometimes."

"Explain that. What do you mean by sometimes?"

The tight end shrugged and let out a sigh of discomfort on the stainless steel bed. "I don't know."

"Let me refresh your memory. You were Ben's fuck buddy, right? No commitment. No loyalty. Just sex. The two of you poked each other with your cocks for fun. You got together and jacked each other off, right? You blew loads together, correct? When you needed a fuck, you called him up and had your way with him, right?"

Davido nodded. Then he said, "You make it sound trashy. It wasn't like that. We have a little more dignity than that."

"How many times did he call you during a week for a good time?" Zane asked.

"Two or three. Sometimes four. It depended on how horny he was. Ben was sexual. The guy enjoyed getting off. But what guy doesn't, right?"

"And how long did that last?"

"Right from the start. Since we met through the league. There was an attraction right from the beginning. When I first moved to town and started playing for the Violators. We hooked up for dinner to get to know each other. We hit it off right away, and ended up screwing each other on a regular basis. Pieney was a good fuck. He knew exactly what to do with his hands, mouth, ass, and cock. If the truth be told, I'm going to miss our bodies mixing together."

"You know a Blaine Phoenix?" Zane was totally on task.

Davido shook his head and rubbed his bottom lip with nervousness. "Never heard of him."

"Ben never mentioned him?"

"Never. His life was pretty private. We didn't talk when we were together, we fucked. That's what our relationship was about. If he wanted a blow job, I was the guy to give it to him, and vice versa. I wasn't the guy he came to for spilling his guts regarding his life. Ben had other people for that, I'm sure."

"Did Ben connect with Jonas Smith, too?" Zane said.

"What do you mean by connect?" Davido furrowed his brows.

My partner cocked his fist up to his mouth and let out a

short cough. He cleared his throat. "Were Ben and Jonas fuck buddies?"

"Like I said, Ben was private. Our relationship consisted of no baggage. It was nice while it lasted and I'll miss it now that he's gone."

"You ever see Ben with Jonas?"

"They're teammates. Of course I saw them together."

"Intimately?" Zane said.

"If they were, it was none of my business. I'm sure Ben fucked around with a lot of guys. I wasn't his secretary and didn't know what he did when we weren't together."

"You lying to me, Cheswick?"

"I don't lie. I'm a good Catholic man who goes to church every Sunday morning. Just because I blow guys and let them use my ass for fun doesn't mean I'm a liar."

Zane asked, "On the night Ben was murdered, where were you at three o'clock in the morning?"

Davido thought about it for a second and said, "Here... getting fucked."

"Can you prove that?"

"Happy's a witness. I think he'd remember seeing me."

"Happy would lie for anyone if he was paid enough," Zane said.

"Cameras are all over this place. You check them out. Surveillance can prove I was here having the time of my life."

"I'll do that," Zane responded. "You spend a lot of time here?"

"Enough. My libido is unstoppable. I like sex with a lot of different guys. This place is my home away from home, besides the field, of course."

"You and Ben ever come here for a good time?" asked Zane.

"Once or twice. He wasn't into it that much. I already said the guy was private."

"Did you ever see Jonas Smith here?"

Davido shook his head and said, "No."

Zane's questions had come to an end. A burly guy with too many earrings, tattoos, and muscles walked into the room. The roughneck slid beside me, reached out with his right hand, and fingered one of my nipples. The dude growled with contentment and removed his towel, which he dropped to the floor. He then stepped into the bath, made some heavy eye contact with me, and said, "There's enough room for you, pretty boy. Why don't you get in here and ride my cock?"

"You've got some great taste in men, pal, but pretty boy is already taken." Zane snatched up my right hand, spun me on my heels, and exited the room with me at his side.

❖

On our return trip to the cruiser, I said to Zane, "I changed my mind."

"How so? Spill your guts. What's up?"

"I think it would be kind of sexy and fun to have a date in there with you. What do you think?"

"You've seen too much cock today. I think you need to get laid, and I'm your guy, if you want it."

"Come to think of it, your cock is the only one I really want."

"Nicely said. Flattery will get you anywhere with me, Troy."

We made the walk back to his cruiser. Once seated inside, he said he was hungry and needed some lunch.

I made a joke and asked, "What are you hungry for? Cowboy or mechanic?"

"Barney's Deli on Poplar Street has a killer Reuben."

"With a pickle on the side?"

"Two…if you're a good boy."

"I'm always a good boy, Zane. You know I love my pickles."

"You're not telling me anything I don't already know, pal."

My cell phone rang and I saw it was Mother; she was probably ready to vent about Cody's new female interest. I took the call as Zane headed for the deli. "Mother?"

"You don't have to sound so rude." She was curt.

"I'm occupied at the moment. Can I call you back?"

"Absolutely not, Troy. I'm just as busy as you are. Don't sound so important."

"What do you need?"

"Troy, don't use that tone with me. How many times do I have to tell you not to raise your voice at me."

"I didn't raise my voice. Now, tell me why you're calling."

"The salon is open again. Umberto just received a call. She informed him the place can open. I just happened to be passing by, heading to Monticello's for some Italian bread, when Umberto called me on my cell phone. He said he tried to reach you but couldn't. Umberto is going over to the salon and you need to meet him there."

"I'm sure that if he needs me, he'll call."

She huffed and said, "There's that tone again. And to think I raised you better. Show your mother some respect. Stop acting like an imbecile."

"Yes, Mother." I sighed.

"And I assume you're sorry, right?"

I rolled my eyes, took a deep breath, and decided to play her game. "I'm sorry, Mother. I won't let it happen again."

"Good. I know it won't. Now, I must run. Things to do. Places to go. I'd rather not bore you with the details."

I was about to tell her good-bye, but she had already clicked off her phone, gone temporarily—until she had a new bitch, of course. Whatever.

I told Zane, "The shop is open. Mother heard from Umberto. I guess the police have fully cleared the place to reopen for business."

"That should keep you busy," Zane said.

"Not like Umberto. He does the hair. I do the books and sale promotions. It works out best that way."

"You never thought of doing hair?" Zane asked. He kept his hands on the cruiser's steering wheel and headed east.

"Never. I prefer bookkeeping over snotty queens with split ends and robust tempers because of bad hair dye."

Zane let out a comfortable laugh and turned his head toward me. He asked, "How about detective work?"

I laughed and patted his leg. "I must admit, I'm partial to dicks."

"Good answer." He laughed again and continued our trip to Barney's Deli.

❖

We were approximately three blocks from our lunch when Zane got an official call on his cellular. Zane chose not to use the speakerphone on his Nextel so I couldn't hear what was being said; some things were not for my civilian ears, of course. After their private conversation, he informed me, "We're going to have to pass on lunch."

I said sarcastically, "That sounds like a typical date for me. A quick gig in a bathhouse, nothing to eat, no kiss, and the date is over."

"Cort Pieney's body was found in his apartment approximately ten minutes ago. Neck is sliced open like his brother's. It's a bloody mess."

"Shit, another body," I said, and promptly lost my appetite.

Zane peered at me and made a U-turn on Pill Street. He said, "It looks like things are just getting started with this case. I hope you're into dick work like you said you were, because we're heading over to Cort's apartment right now."

CHAPTER TEN
IVAN, THE NOT-SO-GREAT

I really didn't want to see a sliced-and-diced Cort Pieney on his living room floor. Panic sort of settled into my thinking and I yelled out to Zane, "Pull over!"

The detective slammed on the brakes, held on to the steering wheel with both hands, and turned his attention to me. Fully concerned, he asked, "What the fuck was that about?"

"Look, I've had a really great time playing detective and all. Now that the salon is open, though, I have to get back there. My responsibilities are calling me."

"Are you dumping me?"

I reached out, touched his right cheek, and said, "That's not it at all. Our date is over for now. We can have another one soon. My life is calling me back. Umberto will expect things done at the shop and—"

"Enough," Zane said, pressed two fingers against my lips. "I understand. I'm just being greedy. I enjoy spending my time with you. This adventure's been fun. And like the old cliché goes, all good things must come to an end."

I pulled his fingers away from my lips. "I'm glad you understand. To be totally honest with you, I really don't want to visit Cort Pieney's crime scene. I'm a rookie at this and don't think my stomach will be able to handle the rough stuff."

"Of course it won't," he agreed. "If I've crossed a line,

Troy, I'm sorry." Again, he supplied his puppy-dog eyes. Shame on him for using that secret weapon on me.

"It's not that," I replied, and shook my head. "You really didn't cross a line. I've done what I can handle. I've enjoyed this escapade with you, but now I have to help Umberto and get the salon running again."

He winked at me. "I'll be a gentleman and drive you to the shop. It's the least I can do."

I shook my head. "That's ridiculous. Nina's expecting you. The shop is over fifteen blocks from here. I'll get a cab."

He pulled the cruiser off Mont Street and parked in a local convenience store. He asked, "Are you sure about this?"

"Positive. Don't feel guilty over it. I'm a big boy and it's my decision." I opened the passenger door.

He reached for my left hand and grazed my fingers with his own. He whispered my name and suggested, "Tomorrow night…we should have a real date. Dinner and a walk. A couple drinks at Hula's. Maybe some dancing, too. What do you think?"

I leaned into the cruiser, kissed him good-bye with my eyes closed, pulled away, and said, "I'll call you, Zane. Let's not rush into this."

❖

Umberto had things up and rolling at the shop, which was no surprise. The man was always on task. Two female clients were already seated in stations four and two. Christina Rotunda, one of our best colorists, waited on one of the clients while Commodore Taylor, a nail artist specialist who just happened to be fabulous with hair, serviced the other female client.

Kitty Carmen, a local blond bombshell with a hip-hop

voice, sang her latest single from the jukebox. Umberto had coffee prepared for the female clients. Upon my entrance, he handed me a martini with two olives and a checklist of chores, and immediately said to me, "I need to see you in our office, pronto."

Umberto closed the office door behind us, told me to gulp my martini down because I was going to need it, and grasped my left forearm. He peered into my pupils like a discontented soothsayer and said, "I have some shocking news for you."

"What's going on? You seem upset, and I need to know why."

"Sit down. I can't tell you this while you're standing."

I sat in the leather chair behind our shared desk. "I'm all ears. Explain what's happening."

Umberto leaned across the desk and removed the toothpick that held my two olives. He tongued them off the pick, chewed them up, and swallowed the pair in a flat second. He commanded, "Take a deep breath and try to find your Zen."

"What for? What's going on? I demand to know. You're acting strange and beginning to freak me out." Fuck it. I downed the martini in two gulps.

He stood straight up, closed his eyes, tilted his head back, and said, "That flake Luanne Ringle is on her way over here to see you. She rattled off some choice words about your involvement with Ivan again."

"What involvement is she talking about?"

He snapped, "That's exactly what I want to know, Troy."

"Stop looking at me that way. There is no involvement with Ivan."

"Because if you were involved with him, you'd tell me, right?"

"Of course."

"Just to make this clear, are you fucking Ivan?"

I shook my head and said, "Absolutely not! You'd be the first to know if I were."

He sighed heavily with relief, patted his heart, crossed himself, and said, "Luanne is pissed out of her mind. What do we do?"

"You handle our clients and let me handle her."

"Outside, I hope?"

"Certainly. I'll meet her on the sidewalk."

He shifted around the desk in a dramatic sweep, patted my head like I was a little cat, and said, "You're a good boy, Charlie Brown."

"I know. Thanks for looking out for me."

"It's the least I can do, darling. Thanks for the olives."

❖

I was too late. Luanne Ringle burst through Umberto's front door with fury in her eyes. She swung a faux Prada from her right arm, clicked her Nine Wests over the tile, and yelped like a banshee, "Where the fuck is that bastard? I know he's here!" She rushed over the black-and-white marble flooring, passed the brushed-aluminum stations, and entered the office.

My partner bolted from the room and carefully steered clear of Luanne and her rage. He snapped the door closed behind him and swished away as if there was a shoe sale at Macy's.

Luanne hissed at him as he passed. She showed off her lipstick-covered fangs and inhuman claws, and (I swear) her red hair rose in spikes on her head.

"Luanne," I said in a calm tone behind my desk, "what brings you to Umberto's?"

"I'll make this short and sweet," she said from the opposite side of the desk.

"I appreciate that. I'm sure you're very much aware that the salon has been closed for two days, which leaves me with a lot of work to catch up on."

She careened straight to her point. "Ivan is my lover! Keep your paws off him!" She opened her purse and pulled out a 9mm, which she aimed at my forehead.

The gun wasn't loaded, I assumed; she didn't have the nerve to rush into a QV business with a loaded weapon. In truth, I should have been scared shitless, but I wasn't. She didn't frighten me, even if she was off her rocker.

"Are you threatening me, Luanne?"

"I have a lot invested in Ivan Reed, which leaves no room for you."

"Our involvement is over. I want nothing to do with him. I've already told you he's yours," I said.

"I don't want to use this on you, Troy. I suggest you behave yourself and don't piss me off. I'm a woman who knows how to use a gun, and will." She twisted the 9mm from left to right in her right. "Men can never be trusted. Especially catty, queer bitches like you. I'm warning you for the final time, Troy. You stay away from my man or I will surely take your balls off with this gun."

I swallowed the saliva at the back of my throat. "I just want to say that you two make a lovely couple, Luanne."

She let out a harrumph and nodded. "I plan to keep it that way. If you fuck this up, Troy, I'll be back. Don't think this isn't loaded. And don't think I won't use it on you, because God knows I will."

She tucked the weapon away, closed her purse, and said, "Good day, Mr. Murdock."

"Okay," was all I could respond with, and watched her do a half spin on her heels as she exited my office.

❖

I must have been pale after Luanne's visit because Umberto walked into the office, gasped, and asked, "Jesus, Troy, what did she do to you?"

I intended to share no details with my business partner because his plate of responsibilities was already heaped with things to accomplish: two stylists called in sick, a third down with a summer flu, and two clients complained of bad cuts, a no-no in our business. The last thing he needed to hear was that my life was in danger and Luanne Pringle was ready to pluck me out of the world with a bullet or two.

One of the staff saved me and popped her head into the office. "Troy, turn on the local news. Some journalist is talking about you again."

Umberto powered up the nineteen-inch LG flat screen in our office and found Channel 11. A reporter stood in front of Cort Pieney's apartment and spoke into the camera with an emphasis on every word: "The Cutie Pie Killer strikes a second time." She informed her audience that Cort Pieney's throat had been slashed and another *Cutie Pie Must Die!* pin was discovered in his mouth. Tara also informed her viewers that I was a suspect.

"Christ," Umberto whispered. His right palm found my back and rubbed along my spine. "You have to reach Zane and get this cleared up. Your life is going to ruins and you need all the help you can get. Plus, our business is going to flop if this drama continues. Something has got to be done about these murders."

"I don't even know where to begin," I said, but sounded like I pitied myself.

"Julie Andrews says to start at the very beginning, or something like that."

I reached for my cell phone on the desk and dialed Zane's number. I listened to his voicemail message and waited to leave a message. Following a long beep, I said, "Zane, it's Troy. I need your help. The media's killing me. Give me a call as soon as possible."

"I must admit, it's nice to have a boyfriend as a detective." Umberto patted my right shoulder.

"He's not my boyfriend. We're just friends helping each other out."

"Friends with benefits?" Umberto questioned with raised eyebrows.

I scowled at him.

"Darling," he said, and waved a finger at me, "I'm just saying he would make a nice boyfriend for you. That's all."

A minute later I left the office in search of a cappuccino across the street, something sweet, and some fresh air.

❖

Five hours later, Zane hadn't called. Six hours, I still heard nothing. I stayed in the office, accomplished some work, looked at my cell phone about seven hundred times, and eventually decided to call it a night.

At 10:51 p.m. I locked up the salon, walked up the stairs to my apartment above the salon, and entered at my own risk.

It was nice to be home again.

My apartment's front door was unlocked. The knob twisted in my hand and the door clicked open. I thought about bolting away and calling Zane for his assistance. Instead, I decided to proceed, having no clue what dangers lurked inside.

Unfortunately, I had returned the stun gun to Zane and was now without a weapon. I had my fists and feet, but come on…I certainly wasn't Vin Diesel. Once inside my living room, I called, "Who's in here? I have a weapon. Show yourself before I become dangerous." It sounded ridiculous, nothing like those action-packed movies starring Matt Damon. Zane would have laughed at my foolishness. Calmly, I walked through the living room toward the kitchen. The apartment was small, and Umberto said it was hugely overdecorated. I skirted around the coffee table, between two identical end tables carved out of maple, and worked my way into the kitchen. I stopped dead in my tracks when I smelled the strong aroma of tobacco. On the opposite side of the room, I saw the shadow of a figure standing by the granite counter. Gray-black smoke wafted through the darkness.

"Ivan," I said, "what are you doing here?"

"How did you know it was me?"

"Your shadow is lanky. Plus, Umberto and you are the only ones with keys to this apartment." I flicked on the kitchen light.

Ivan yelled, "She can't see me here! Turn out the light!"

I flicked the kitchen light off and asked, "What the fuck's going on, Ivan? Why are you playing this game with me?"

"I didn't mean to startle you, Troy. A man just needs to find some seclusion from those maniacs in the world."

I semi-grinned in the dark, knowing he was talking about Luanne. I leaned into the wall with my left shoulder, tired beyond belief, and sighed heavily. "Spill the beans, buddy. Fill me on your drama. I've got time."

He cleared his throat, took another drag of his cigarette, exhaled, and said, "We need to talk. You're in trouble and I think I can help you."

He could help? How? Ivan had his own problems and didn't need to interfere with mine. A yawn escaped, then two yawns, and I asked, "What kind of trouble are you talking about?"

"Luanne Ringle trouble."

"Shit." I rolled my eyes in the dark. "Start talking. I'm listening."

❖

We moved through the dark and found ourselves in my living room on the lime-green vinyl sofa I'd picked up at a garage sale two summers before. Ivan sat on one end of the sofa and I sat on the opposite end. I asked him if he wanted something strong to drink, which he declined. He claimed he had a problem with drinking and his stomach, and now attended Alcoholics Anonymous meetings.

"I know Luanne visited you this afternoon at the salon." Warm yellow light glowed within the room and Ivan sat motionless, holding my knife, in my favorite reading spot.

"Word gets around fast." I yawned. Damn, I needed to go to bed. Fatigue had set into my mind and muscles.

"I'm afraid she has a mind of her own. Luanne has no control at times. Her dramas are always extreme, no matter the situation." He stubbed out his cigarette in an ash tray and dug for a second menthol inside his shirt pocket. He lit it with his Zippo and took a drag. "The woman's at full tilt. She has the potential to hurt herself, and others."

I knew that firsthand and said, "She doesn't have to hurt me in the meantime. Luanne Ringle's a whacko, Ivan. There's a lot of negative things I could say about her, but I feel it's a waste of time. The woman needs to be institutionalized or on some heavy medication. Something is surely not clicking right inside her gears."

"Luanne is very smart and knows how to work the system to get what she wants. Trust me, she takes plenty of drugs, which probably also causes her to be dangerous."

"She's threatened me twice."

He took a fresh drag on his cigarette and filled the living room with smoke. He said, "I know...I know. This is the trouble with Luanne. If things aren't going her way, she goes semi-postal."

"She's at full throttle, baby. There's nothing that's going to bring her sanity back from this point on."

"The guy that was following me the other night just might do that," he confessed.

"The redhead in the black Mustang?" I asked, caught off guard by his statement.

"Yes. That's him. He's a friend of Luanne's. They see the same therapist in Rockford Square. That's where they met."

"Luanne knows him?"

"I think she does. Luanne knows a lot of people. Her circle of friends and acquaintances is quite large."

"Who is he? And why was he following you?"

"Bernie Bottle. He's just looking out for Luanne's safety. He doesn't want anyone to hurt Luanne."

"Does he know Luanne's your girlfriend?"

He shook his head and frowned at me. "She's not my girlfriend. You've always assumed she was. We are merely friends. We have always been just friends. I can't possibly have a loon like her in my life. She'd drive me crazy."

"If I remember correctly, you left me for her."

"Wrong," Ivan said. "We had a mutual breakup."

"I have to disagree. You left me without telling me you

were leaving. I woke up one morning alone and all your things were gone. I then found out from a mutual friend of ours that you were staying with Luanne and…"

Silence ensued for a few seconds. I heard traffic on Manndon Street. A horn blew.

"My visit here this evening isn't about you and me. It's about Luanne and Bernie Bottle."

I don't know how long my heart raced within my chest and the space between my temples buzzed. Eventually I calmed down. It was time for a needed drink, but I was too tired to fetch one. "What about Luanne?" I asked.

"There's no sense in hiding the obvious, Troy. Luanne has made it quite clear to the both of us that she wants you out of the picture."

"What do you mean by that?"

"Gone. Vanished. She says you rub her the wrong way."

"How can I do that when I don't even know her?"

"Exactly. Just stay calm and listen to me."

"Who takes care of her since she's a basket case?"

"She has no family that I'm aware of. Luanne has herself…and me. I found myself helping her after I left you."

"That's correct. You left me. And by the sounds of it, you need to choose better friends, Ivan. Does Bernie Bottle help take care of her, too?"

He nodded. "Whenever he can. He's a busy guy and protects a lot of people."

For some strange reason I remembered my Jeep being torched. Something clicked within my head and I blurted, "Luanne is the one who set my Jeep on fire, isn't she?"

"I don't know that for sure. I'm just here to tell you that Luanne has a lot of problems. She's schizophrenic and doesn't know what she does half the time. I didn't come here to cause any problems for you."

"What, while she's murdering me?"

"That's not funny. Show a bit of compassion."

"Can you stop her?" I asked.

"I don't believe so. Discussing her drama only heightens her anger."

"Do you want to stop her?"

"Why wouldn't I want to stop her?"

I paused, craving alcohol. Ivan ruining me was always a possibility. The days following his disappearance from my apartment were ugly. We had grown out of love, became distant with each other, and...

"What are you thinking about?"

"Nothing," I responded.

"Now you're lying to me."

I closed my eyes and shook my head. "I was thinking you might be using Luanne to get revenge on me for our failed relationship."

He chuckled. "That's the most ridiculous thing I've ever heard. Revenge? Come on, Troy, we're not in high school. The woman suffers from mental illness. Our relationship ended two years ago."

"I can easily see you using a mentally deranged somebody to carry out your war against me. Toss some Bernie Bottle into the mix, too, just for the fuck of it."

"That's bullshit and you know it." Ivan glared at me.

"How do I know it's bullshit?"

Ivan quickly moved over to my side of the couch, sliding across the vinyl. He grasped my right hand within his left one and confessed, "I believe I'm still in love with you, Troy Murdock."

"But you left me high and dry," I said, still hurt after two years.

"I'm sorry about that. I should have never left. I was confused. I thought we were going too fast. I thought…"

"I thought this was about Luanne Ringle?" I asked, confused.

"It is about Luanne…and us, a little."

Ivan tried to kiss me, but I pushed him away. "Can we leave the us part out of it?"

"I suppose we could," Ivan said. He slid back over to the other side of the couch, extinguished his cigarette, crossed his arms over his chest, and asked, "Will you walk me to the door?"

"I can't do that," I responded. "I'm just going to sit here and take in everything you have said. You can walk yourself out, if you don't mind."

Ivan was at my side in a matter of seconds, mussed my hair with his right palm, leaned over, and kissed the top of my head. When he finally pulled away from me, he said, "Watch out for her, Troy. Luanne's a very dangerous woman. I don't want you to get hurt because of her."

"I'll watch my back, Ivan."

"I'll watch it, too."

While he left my apartment, I thought, *You want to watch more than my back, Ivan Reed. Sorry I don't feel the same way.*

CHAPTER ELEVEN
IN TOO DEEP

The next morning Zane surfaced in my apartment. Throughout that slow period of waking, I smelled wheat and butter pancakes, fresh coffee, and sausages sizzling in a frying pan. He walked around the apartment in a pair of cotton briefs. I climbed out of bed and stretched, walked to the tiny breakfast nook/kitchen area that overlooked the back alley, and heard him say, "I hope you don't mind, I broke in this morning and decided to use your washer. Mine is on the fritz." He passed me a mug of steamy coffee and kissed my left cheek, which I enjoyed. Slowly he pulled away from me and said, "Damn, you are so hot in the morning. I particularly like the mussed-hair look and dawn stubble."

"You're not so bad either."

Another kiss, this time on my neck. The sausages needed turning and he left my side to rescue them. At the stove, in his briefs, he held a spatula and said, "I took care of the media for you. You're out of their scope for the time being. I sent them on a hunt for a pedophile named Marvin C. Tuft, who will keep them busy for a little while."

"Thank you," I said. I sipped my coffee. "You're a dream boy."

The sausages were done, as well as the pancakes. I sat down at the two-person table set with Ikea plates and flatware, butter, maple syrup, and strawberry preserves. He served me two pancakes and three sausages. "You need a power breakfast today. We have lots of work to do. I want to pay Coach Bassett a visit, and two of Cort's friends."

"I can't go with you today. I need to work at the salon this morning. Besides, my mother expects me for lunch." I took another sip of coffee and peered across the table.

"How about I talk to Coach Bassett this morning and you work in the salon? Afterward, we hook up at your mother's for lunch."

I shook my head. "You are not visiting Mother. She knows you tried to kill me three times and she'll go ballistic if you step a foot in her house."

"Accidents happen. I'm sure she can understand that." He shared a look with me that said *I'm trying here, stop being a queen.*

I rolled my eyes. "Mother understands nothing. She's a viper...and very protective of her two boys. Lunch is not a possibility."

"I'll charm and woo her with my detective skills."

"She'll eat you up and spit you out. Mother has no genial side." I slipped a forkful of pancake lathered with butter and syrup into my mouth.

"That's too bad, I was hoping to meet her."

"Never," I said with my mouth full, enjoying the pancakes.

Zane stood, walked over to my side, and said, "You have syrup on your bottom lip. Let me get that." He licked my bottom lip in a frisky and sexy manner, then kissed me, pulled off and backed away from my lips, and said, "I wore this outfit just for you this morning, Troy. What do you think?"

I didn't have syrup on my bottom lip. Nor was his washer

on the fritz. Helplessly, I kissed him back, found three fingers over the middle of his cotton briefs, and allowed him to escort me to the couch, where we toyed with each other for the next hour.

❖

A few hours later, I said to Umberto, "I'm a whore."

He had taken a moment out to wash and trim my hair; I never argued with the best hairdresser in town. The salon was closed for the next hour, which gave him plenty of time to make me handsome. "As long as you're a happy whore," he said and scissored a few unneeded curls away from the nape of my neck.

"What do you mean by that?"

"I think Mr. Dick makes you happy. You're glowing."

"I am not glowing."

"Trust me, darling...you're glowing. I've seen it a million times."

"He's too dangerous for me. I can't get involved with a guy who carries a gun around for a living."

Another snip. Umberto stepped away from his work of art and admired the back of my head. "We all have guns, darling. Some of us just don't know how to use them. Apparently, Mr. Ward is very skilled in the gun-handling area."

"That's not funny," I said. "And I'm still a whore."

"I hate to say it, sweetheart, you're already involved with him. The two of you are getting serious and you don't even realize it. Take it for what it's worth and run with it. A guy like Zane Ward is hard to find."

❖

Ivan Reed called and asked for me. Umberto answered the phone, placed Ivan on hold, found me counting Virago hair spray bottles in the inventory closet. Upon his entrance, he said, "Sweeties, once you get out of the closet, stay out. There's no reason for you to slip back inside."

"We're missing seven bottles of hair spray."

"We are not missing anything. I took them home the other night. One must stock up to look this beautiful." He waved a palm around his face in a comical manner.

"You have to tell me when you do things like that, Umberto. I was about to place blame on a thieving employee."

"You've got bigger problems to worry about, babe. The phone's for you." He presented the slimline Panasonic to me, but I decided not to take it right away.

"Who is it?"

"Ivan Reed. The man wants you back. Obviously, he's not going to give up until he has you again."

"What does he want?"

"Come on, Troy, that one's easy. Ivan wants to be the mother of your children. Now, get out of the closet and talk to him. I'm not holding this phone all fucking day."

I exited the closet and took the portable from him. I said, "Ivan?" in a pleasant manner.

Umberto stood at my side. His head leaned against mine as he eavesdropped on my conversation.

Ivan said, "I took the gun away from her, Troy."

"What? Who?" The two questions flew out of me with ease.

"Luanne. I took the gun away from her. She confessed about threatening you yesterday. Someone had to take the gun from her."

"Praise the Lord and pass the ammunition," I said. "She's

insane, Ivan. I highly suggest you drop her as a friend and move on with your life."

"Speaking of moving on, Troy, I want to see you tonight."

"That's not possible. I'm busy."

"We can share a nice dinner and a movie together...like old times."

"Although the invitation is very flattering, I don't think I'm up for that."

"Just you and me."

"Ivan, look...we're not the couple of the year. You need to find a way of letting me go. I'm not your knight in shining armor. Find an online site and start dating a bear."

He sobbed on the phone. It wasn't the first time I'd made a guy cry; it certainly wouldn't be the last. Sometimes I had to be emotionally brutal to get my point across. Since he was hardheaded about our nonexistent relationship, I found it easy to blow him off. Good for me.

"I'm hanging up now, Ivan."

"Don't go," he faintly whispered.

"I'm sorry," I said, pulled the phone away from my ear, and pressed the Off button.

Umberto looked at me. He shrugged his shoulders, smiled, and said, "Men...They can be the biggest babies."

"Exactly," I agreed.

❖

Mother had prepared mint iced tea, chimichurri wraps, and sides of fruit salad for lunch. Cody was present, minus Liz Bradbaum. I arrived late by fifteen minutes, a big no-no in the Murdock menagerie. Minnie was in a splendid mood, though.

A basket of sunflowers and her favorite chocolates had arrived approximately one hour before.

Cody, who arrived on time and sucked up to Mother, asked, "Who are the flowers and chocolates from?"

"Detective Zane Ward. Troy's friend. He should be here any minute. I've invited him to lunch."

My jaw dropped with surprise. What was one supposed to do in that situation? And what was Zane up to? He probably had every intention of finding himself wrapped around Mother's little finger. His charm was unlimited, and his smile could woo just about anyone.

"He's late," Cody said.

I shrugged my shoulders.

Mother said, "Detective Ward is a very busy man. Of course he's running late. The man protects our city and serves our community. That's more than I can say for my own sons."

"He tried to kill Troy three times. Do you remember that, Mother?" Cody attempted to stoke Mother's rage.

I kicked him under the table and nailed his tibia with some force. Honestly, it felt great to accomplish that. Cody always tried to cause conflict at mealtimes, which just about threw me over the edge of sanity and brought out the demon in me.

"Accidents happen, Cody. Detective Ward is a very nice man. Plus, he's so handsome. A peach. I adore him."

Gross. My mother had just admitted to having a slight crush on my friend. I wanted to vomit. I felt uncomfortable, and really just wanted to wrap up lunch and leave.

My older brother gloated across the table from me. The doorbell rang. Mother excused herself from the dining room table and fetched my so-called boyfriend from the front porch.

Zane entered the room with a beaming smile. He shook Cody's hand and said, "A pleasure to see you again."

Mother entered the room behind Zane. "Please make yourself comfortable next to Troy."

As Zane sat down at the table, he rubbed his left palm against my right thigh under the table. I met with him with a gaze that said *Not in front of my family. Don't cross a line.*

Zane cheerily said, "Long time no see, Troy. Wasn't it kind of your mother to invite me for lunch?"

Mother glowed and filled Detective Ward's plate with a wrap and a small bowl of fruit salad.

"This looks delicious, Mrs. Murdock," Zane said, and took a generous sip of his iced tea. Act or no act, Zane was awesome at winning my mother over. He knew exactly what strings to pull and provided the sincere endearments she wanted to hear.

"Call me Minnie." Mother beamed with angelic lightness.

My brother rolled his eyes. Cody was ready to explode with anger. He took a bite of his chimichurri wrap, chewed it up quickly, and swallowed it.

Zane laid it on pretty thick. As he also consumed his wrap, he told Mother, "Your hair looks marvelous. What are you using in it?"

Again, I rolled my eyes; obviously, it was my turn.

Cody dropped his napkin to the table. "Mother, I have to go."

"So soon? You barely touched your lunch, sweetheart." Minnie steered her view away from Zane.

"Yes. I have things to do." It was a blatant lie; all of us could see it in Cody's eyes. The poor bastard couldn't lie as a child, and he was no better at it as a full-grown adult.

"What things?" Mother asked.

"Just things!" Cody barked, and peered at me with daggers in his handsome eyes.

"Suit yourself," Mother said in a prissy and belittling manner, and added, "Zane, could you pass the honey mustard, please? My wrap is just a little bit dry."

Cody bolted like a seven-year-old, which I felt bad about, but I said nothing to stop him. Instead, I watched Zane pass the honey mustard to Mother and listened to him say, "Your hair, Minnie…I just love the wave in it. Now, tell me what you've been using."

❖

Post-lunch, Zane and I walked out of Mother's house, down the cobblestone sidewalk, and ended up at his cruiser. "What the hell was that about?"

"What are you talking about?"

"You sounded like an ass in there. When did you really give a shit about my mother's hair?"

"You're overthinking this, Troy. I was being kind and thoughtful. Every woman needs to hear a few compliments over lunch. What is so wrong with that? I was just trying to be a gentleman."

"You overdid it. Even Cody knew that. He's not stupid. Why do you think he left so abruptly?"

"He was inferior to my good looks and felt out of place."

"That's not funny," I barked, and punched him in his right shoulder.

He rubbed his shoulder and said, "My goal was for Minnie to like me. I think I succeeded. As for your brother, he's not the one I like to fuck, kiss, and squeeze against me, so I really don't give a shit about how he feels regarding my lunch with his mother."

I pulled away from him and huffed.

Zane ignored me and walked around the cruiser, which was parked across the street from the '88 Buick I'd borrowed from Mr. Tibet.

I yelled at his back, "You pissed off my brother! What do you have to say for yourself?"

He turned around at his cruiser's door and faced me like a man. His expression said he wasn't thrilled with how things were currently working out between us: furrowed brows, anguished eyes, wrinkles around his lips. "He's a big boy and he'll get over it."

"You've crossed a line, Detective Ward."

"It's my job to cross lines. Besides, I've done worse things than piss off a brother."

His cell phone buzzed at his hip, the theme song from *Raiders of the Lost Ark*. He unclipped it from his side, looked at the number, flipped the phone open, and asked, "What's going on?"

I stood patiently by the passenger door and waited for his conversation to end. In the meantime, I heard a lot of affirmatives out of Zane, one *absolutely not*, and an *I'm on my way there*. Zane disconnected his call and demanded, "Get in. I need your help."

"What kind of help?"

"Just get in and stop with the shit!"

I opened the passenger door, climbed inside, and said, "This better be good, Zane Ward...or Mother Minnie's going to pull a Charlie Manson on you."

"Your mother couldn't step on an ant, Troy, and you know it."

"Perhaps. But she's pretty good at turning my boyfriends into eunuchs. Just so you know, of course."

He laughed and said, "Thanks for the warning. I'll keep my balls under close care."

❖

We drove to Manchester Park on the west side of town. Zane parked the cruiser in front of 78239 Manchester Drive, climbed out, and instructed me to follow him.

Manchester Park was a neighborhood filled with Tudor-style homes where a selection of professors from Quill Village College—which was three blocks away—lived. The properties all looked the same: cobblestone walkways, white picket fences, and manicured lawns. We walked up to a red door without a window and he asked over his right shoulder, "You need a gun?"

"I don't do guns, Zane."

"You do guys with guns," he challenged.

"And well," I added, bragging a bit.

"Absolutely. That's why we hang out together." He looked serious. "This might get ugly. I just want to warn you of that."

"Why's it going to get ugly?"

"Watch and learn, guy."

Zane tapped on the red door three times. The door opened and a shirtless middle-aged man with a goatee, gray eyes, and nipple rings responded with a sharp "What?"

Detective Ward's badge was flashed and Zane said, "Quill Village Police, Mr. Tuft. I have a couple questions for you."

Tuft said, "Fuck off!" and attempted to push the door closed.

Zane blocked the door with his left foot. He pulled a gun

out of his jeans at the small of his back and pushed the door open.

I was scared shitless and had no clue what was going down. Before I knew it, Zane was inside the house, and I followed behind.

Once inside, Tuft popped off a shot and missed my head by three inches. Quickly, while I ducked, I saw Tuft stood on the opposite side of the cluttered living room with a Smith and Wesson 78G.

Zane pushed me to the floor and yelled, "Down!"

The sound of a second shot filled the room.

Zane shot at Tuft, missed, and said, "Put the fucking gun down!"

Tuft fired off a third shot. Zane fired a second shot, missing Tuft again. What the fuck was going on? Didn't Zane graduate from the police academy? Detectives were supposed to hit their targets, for Christ's sake. What the hell?

I shuddered on the floor and believed my life as a businessman was over. My heart raced and sweat formed on my forehead and under my arms.

Zane pulled at my shirt and said, "Get up, Troy! He's going out the back!"

I couldn't move, though. An abundance of terror had surfaced within my world and I became numb, unable to move, and almost lifeless on the dirty floor.

Zane took off after Tuft. He dashed through the living room like a superhero and left me behind.

Not seven seconds later I heard a gun go off in the backyard, followed by a masculine scream. At first, I wasn't sure who got shot, but then Tuft called out at the top of his voice, "You fucking shot me, pig! You fucking shot me!"

❖

In the next thirty minutes I learned that Marvin C. Tuft was into kiddie porn and had a naked twelve-year-old boy tied with leather straps to his queen-size bed on the second floor. Tuft also had a computer in his office, which was filled with pornographic pics of boys in bondage, a diary filled with boys' names, phone numbers, and addresses, victims he had sexually molested—sure signs that he wouldn't be released from prison anytime soon.

Zane suffered a minor abrasion to his left cheek from one of Tuft's bullets.

Back at the cruiser, after things calmed down on Manchester Drive, I suggested he go to the hospital and get checked out. Zane refused. He crawled inside the car, scowled at me, and said, "You don't live too far from here, right? You can put a bandage on it at your place. There's no way in hell I'm going to a hospital."

I shook my head and said, "This has to stop."

"What has to stop?"

"This detective thing going on? You almost got me killed back there."

Zane guffawed. "Trust me, that was nothing."

"Nothing is food poisoning. That pedophile was shooting bullets at me. I saw my life flash before my eyes."

"You're exaggerating."

"I'm being normal. I'm being honest. I'm in too deep with you."

"You loved the action and you know it."

I was angry. Bottom line: Zane had placed me in considerable jeopardy and risked my life. I could have been murdered, or severely hurt. As with the few dates we went on before, he was irresponsible, careless, and only thought about himself.

I said, "I didn't, Zane. This incident inside the Tuft house was some serious shit. You put my life in danger. I can't be associated with a guy like that."

"I told you it could get ugly."

"Ugly is having a bad hair day for me. Ugly is not hunting down a pedophile and shooting him in the arm."

He sighed heavily. He grabbed his temples with both palms and closed his eyes over the steering wheel.

"I'll get a cab from here. Or Umberto can come and pick me up."

"Honestly, I can drive you back to your apartment."

I shook my head and exited his cruiser. "No thanks. I'm going to end up dead hanging around you. The first three times were accidents, but this one wasn't."

He leaned across the cruiser's front seat and begged, "Come on, Troy. You're being melodramatic. You're being—"

I hustled away and entered Manchester Park on my walk home, back to my apartment. Nine city blocks wasn't that far, was it? Maybe a walk would numb some of the anger inside my core. No matter what, Zane and I were no longer involved, as far as I was concerned. That wasn't going to change, I promised myself—honestly.

CHAPTER TWELVE
A MAN IN HEELS

"Coach Bassett's on the chopping block, baby doll," Umberto explained to me as he watched a clip on the evening news in his apartment. He lounged on his favorite leather Italian recliner, relaxing after a hard day's work at the salon. The guy wasn't really lazy, but he did know how to kick back and enjoy his time.

Axel sat cross-legged on the floor in front of the recliner. He was massaging his Cuban lover's feet with a top-of-the-line cocoa butter.

I was at Umberto's side, was drinking a margarita with no salt in an attempt to soothe my nerves. I sucked down some of the alcohol and said, "Coach Bassett is not human. I would hate to have him on my ass."

"He's straight, conchita. Bassett would not want to be on your ass," my business partner replied.

The scene on the television showed Bassett exiting Tarton Field and heading toward his Escalade in the parking lot. Coyne Masters, one of WQQV's sexiest reporters (think gay Clark Kent), was at Bassett's side, and asked the coach of the Quill Village Violators, "Do you have an alibi?"

Bassett tried to cover his face with his right hand and shook his head. "No comment!"

"Did you have anything to do with the Pieney murders?" Masters positioned his microphone against Bassett's right hand.

Coach Bassett abruptly pushed the mike away. "Again, no comment!"

Masters put it back in the coach's face and asked, "Where do you purchase the *Cutie Pie Must Die!* pins?"

Bassett dashed to his vehicle.

Masters ran after him. He was right at the coach's side with a microphone in a matter of seconds, and asked, "Who's next on your victims list?"

The coach of the Violators had had enough. He climbed inside his Escalade and slammed the driver's door in the reporter's face, knocking the microphone to the asphalt.

As Bassett drove away, Masters said to his viewers, "The two unsolved murders are raising panic in the city. A murderer is still at large. I'm Coyne Masters reporting from Tarton Field. Back to you, Cindy."

Umberto said, "The coach is in deep shit."

"Better him than me," I responded.

❖

I returned home an hour later, ready for a cup of decaf and one sudoku puzzle before bed. I microwaved a mug of Evian water, found a jar of instant decaffeinated coffee, and walked the prepared coffee into my bedroom, where I planned to complete the puzzle.

To my horror, Luanne Ringle sat on the middle of my bed with her ankles crossed. She was wearing a pair of khaki-colored shorts, espadrilles, and a white tank. Her hair was pulled into a tight ponytail and she wore a faint layer of makeup, which showed off her cheekbones.

I dropped the cup and saucer; neither broke, to my surprise.

She said, "You're awfully jittery, Troy. A man with your detective skills shouldn't be that easily startled."

"Luanne," I whispered as my socks absorbed the hot coffee from the floor, "I didn't know you had a key to the place." Clearly, she had stolen Ivan's key right from under his nose.

Luanne replied, "When a woman wants things, she finds a way."

I wondered if she had a gun. If so, how good was her aim? Honestly, I didn't want to find out. I had seven more good lives left in me, and she wasn't about to take any of them away. I asked, "Are you looking for Ivan?"

"I found who I'm looking for." She didn't blink. "I'm upset with you, Troy. It's only right to tell you why."

It was impossible to call 911 since my cell phone was in the kitchen, which felt a million miles away at the moment. The bedroom truly lacked clutter, which prevented me from finding a quick weapon to use. The best thing to do, I reasoned, was to listen, agree with her, and hope she would leave soon without causing much damage to my apartment, or to me.

"Ivan still has a crush on you. I know that for a fact because he talks in his sleep. There are no secrets between us, thanks to his chitter-chatter at night." She paused, perhaps waiting for me to say something in return, which I didn't. "He wants you back, which I'm sure you're very much aware of. He longs for your touch…and whatever else faggots do together, which I really don't want to know about."

"Yes, I know that he still likes me."

"Loves," she corrected me. "Ivan is still in love with you. He won't deny it if you ask him." She examined her manicure. "It's all bullshit, if you ask me, Troy. I don't get this guy-with-guy thing. I'm not a homophobe. But I would be lying if I didn't say it's a bit tedious to understand. Two penises touching sort of grosses me out. No woman would ever find that a turn-on. And the concept of what men do to each other's bottoms...I really want to be left in the dark about that."

"Most straight people do, Luanne." Where was this conversation going? God only knew. Patiently, I kept my poise.

"It's so easy to lose at this game, Troy. You're such a nice guy. I know that I really can't compete with you. Ivan will have you in a second. You have minimal flaws and he thinks you're perfect. Besides, I don't have a cock." She sniffled and wiped tears away with the backs of her well-manicured hands.

I asked, "How did you get here, Luanne?"

"I took a cab."

"That's good to know."

She sniffled. "I mean, I get around a lot. Just because I don't have a vehicle doesn't mean I stay in my apartment all day."

I tried to get to the point, and asked, "Do you want Ivan to come and pick you up?"

She shook her head. "Of course not. I'll walk home."

"That's absurd. It's over a mile. Let me call a cab for you."

She shook her head again and asked, "Could you drive me, please?"

Maybe if I scratched her back, she would scratch mine in the future. I nodded. "I can definitely do that. A woman shouldn't be walking alone at night."

A smile warmed her face and she finally stopped crying. She lightly coughed and said, "You're an angel. No wonder Ivan fell for you. He always did call you a keeper."

❖

The next morning over a croissant and coffee, and with a Brandenburg concerto by Bach on the stereo, I checked my email. Why not? I lived alone and could. Singlehood was nice that way: I never had to look like a supermodel, clutter could accumulate, and I could eat a can of soup for dinner if I wanted to. In truth, I just had to take care of myself. Good for me.

Comfy at my Dell flat screen, I read the first email from Mother. Her subject line said RESPOND ASAP and the email read: *I need to see you. This Beth thing is bothering me. We must stop this now! I cannot permit my son to be involved with that woman. My babies will never get married! Help me stop this!*

I deleted two email ads regarding erectile dysfunction.

Cody's email read: *Mother is a lunatic. Lately, I just can't find myself understanding her. Should we take her to see Dr. Pine? Maybe he could suggest a drug to help her through this phase? Her comments about us never getting married cannot be serious, right? We will never drive buses, Troy! What's gotten into her? We need to focus on her mental health. I'm sure Dr. Pine will know exactly what to prescribe for her.*

The next email subject line said: Need A Jock? Want To Fuck? *No thanks*, I thought, and clicked the Delete button.

Ivan had sent me an email. I couldn't remember the last time that happened. The subject line said Very Sorry. I clicked on the email and read: *Thank you for getting Luanne home safe last night. That was the nicest thing you could have done for her. Obviously, she was in a depressed state when she broke into your apartment, which I apologize for. I really don't know what to do with her. Sometimes her behavior is out of control. Anyway, you're the greatest, again. Thinking of you, Ivan.*

Zane's subject line said Good Morning, Sunshine! and his email read: *You can't hide from me; I won't let you. I'm sorry. I'm sorry. I'm sorry. I'm sorry. Will you ever forgive me about the shooting yesterday? Can I make it up to you? I want to have lunch with you today. I'll pick you up at noon at the salon. Wear a dark suit.*

Wear a dark suit? What was up with that? I rolled my eyes and responded: *Don't get me shot! No more crime scenes! I'll be wearing Kenneth Cole.*

❖

While I undressed for a shower, I called Umberto. I shared information about a schedule change for an employee, Milene Andrews, and inventory changes on a new shipment of hair product by an English company called Lordess Fennie, and told him that chair number six was broken in the shop. I also explained to Umberto that a repairman by the name of Dolf Lindenger was going to stop by to carry out a few chair repairs.

"Is he hot and blond, Troy? You know those are my favorite repairman types."

"I don't know."

"He sounds German. I love Germans, minus Hitler."

"I think he is German."

"I hope he has hair I can run my hands through."

"Let me remind you that you have a boyfriend."

"Running one's hands through a man's sexy hair does not constitute having an affair or having sex. Besides, Axel would be infuriated with me if I didn't flirt with Dolf."

"Whatever," I sighed. "I'll be in after a shower."

"I'll be waiting, darling."

I relaxed in the warm shower for the next twenty minutes

and exited the hot spray to the buzzing sound of my cell phone. After I wrapping a towel around my middle, I found the cell and listened to Mother's rage: "Troy, who does he think he is? Cody should not be involved with a woman!"

"Would you rather he be involved with a man?" Mother Minnie was not homophobic, but sometimes I just had to wonder because of the bizarre things she would say.

"That's not at all funny."

"Calm down, Mother. Why are you outraged?"

"He's serious about Beth, and I refuse to accept it."

"She goes by Liz, Mother, or Elizabeth, whichever you prefer. And you can accept her. We're not boys anymore. We're men who will fall in love. Have you discussed this with Georgina?" Georgina Fitzgerald was another one of Mother's friends. The two women were like sisters.

"Georgina's in Jamaica with Randall. She won't be back until tomorrow."

"Just wait until she returns, then. Georgina will know exactly what to say about Cody and Liz, and help you through this."

"You're siding with Cody, aren't you?"

"Yes." I saw no sense in lying.

"Dammit! You can't do that, Troy."

"I most certainly can."

Mother hung up on me.

❖

Dolf Lindenger was beautiful in every sense of the word. Because the morning was hot, he arrived at the salon in a chest-clinging tank with a lifeguard symbol in the center of his firm pecs. His bulging biceps and chiseled features turned heads, including mine. And he was blond, which turned Umberto into a tongue-wagging little boy who took a fond interest in his... work.

Although Dolf was gorgeous, I had better things to do at the salon. For the next two hours I worked at solving problems: ordering supplies, paying bills, and sending out bills. At approximately eleven thirty, I changed into a black Kenneth Cole suit, Italian loafers, silk tie, and waited patiently for Zane Ward.

Today Zane wasn't driving his cruiser; instead he was driving a black Durango that smelled like a seascape candle. He was dressed in a pinstriped black suit and a ruby-colored silk tie. When I climbed into the passenger seat he kissed me on my left cheek. "I missed you."

"You're sucking up because you almost got me killed yesterday."

"You're clever."

"My mama ain't raised a fool," I joked.

"That's too bad. I rather like fools," he said.

"Enough. Where are we going?"

"A double funeral."

"The Pieney brothers?"

"You got it."

"Just what I wanted for lunch." I rolled my eyes.

"And afterward, there's a wake for the victims at their aunt's."

"Awesome...just how I like my dessert."

❖

The cemetery was quiet, redolent with flowers and trees. Tombstones were scattered here and there. Cars were lined up near a mausoleum, with red-and-yellow FUNERAL banners on their hoods. A group of mourners stood next to the brothers' side-by-side open graves.

"I cannot do this," I clarified in the Durango while observing the grievers. "My stomach is already turning. I do hair, not cemeteries."

"Don't make me drag you out there. We need to pay our respects. Plus, we could learn something."

"Wrong. You need to handle this. I'm just a small business owner."

"As my sidekick today, you're obligated to help me."

I flashed him a look of agitation and said, "You think you're so smart, Detective Ward."

"Get over it. The service is almost ready to start. Climb your ass out of the Durango and do what I do."

I rolled my eyes and ignored him.

❖

The funeral service was outside in the ninety-plus heat; I had pools of perspiration under my pits. Even my briefs were becoming soggy. Friends and relatives of the deceased were sweating to death. Any hotter, and there would have been more bodies to bury.

Mrs. Paula Pieney was surrounded by her family. She looked flushed, drugged, and overwhelmed by the heat. Zane and I stood beside each other, shoulder to shoulder, two rows back from the gravesites. To his right were familiar faces: Coach Bassett, Blaine Phoenix, Jonas Smith, and Davido Cheswick. All were quiet with their heads bowed.

As Father Bowenstack walked his way through the death pageant, I leaned into Zane and said, "Who are you here to question?"

"The blond with the red lipstick. Izzy Shempire. One of Jonas Smith's lovers."

"I thought Jonas only liked guys."

"He does. Izzy's not a woman."

❖

Following the service, we caught Izzy walking to her candy red BMW 1800. Formerly known as Landon Michael Shempire, Izzy was polite enough to stop in the shade and speak with us after Zane flashed his badge. She lit a Virginia Slim and crossed her arms. "I only have a few minutes. I'm expected by one of my clients."

"What do you do, Miss Shempire?" Zane asked.

"I'm in the underwear business. I model some and sell. I'm partners with Charlie Bass. We own Undermen. Have you heard of it?"

"I'm wearing a pair right now," I said.

"Do you like our product?"

"Absolutely. And so does my boyfriend," I said, elbowing Zane in his side.

Miss Shempire smiled and nodded. She took a feminine drag of her cigarette, exhaled, and said, "I love to hear about boyfriends."

"Is Jonas Smith your boyfriend?" Zane asked.

"No." Miss Shempire shook her head. "We don't like labels."

"But you do sleep with him?"

"Yes. Occasionally. He's a very busy man."

"How long have you been intimate with Jonas?"

"One year, something like that. He's mentioned marriage, but I'm not that type of girl."

"Were you friends with Ben Pieney?"

"Oh no. They are all like boys together."

"Who are like boys together?" Zane asked.

"Jonas, Davido, Blaine…and Ben, of course."

"How close of friends were they?"

"They went out twice a week together."

"What did they do together?"

Shempire blushed and batted her eyes. She said, "What all boys do together."

"Any other friends in their group, Miss Shempire?"

"Tab Fuller and Sniper."

"Sniper?" Zane inquired.

"Yes." Shempire nodded. "Ashton Sniper. A nice guy. One of Ben's boyfriends."

Zane lifted an eyebrow. "How many boyfriends did Ben have?"

Shempire said, "I don't know. Ben liked a lot of company. He was never alone. Football was his game and men were his life." She looked down at her glittery diamond Tiffany watch and explained, "I'm sorry, gentlemen, I really have to run."

"Thank you, Miss Shempire. You've been very helpful."

We watched her move out of the shade and climb into her BMW 1800. Shempire waved and drove away.

❖

Back in the Durango, I watched Zane making notes in his notepad. I asked, "Whatcha writing, big boy?"

"We've been lied to by Phoenix, Jonas, and Davido. They're all friends. Obviously Ben didn't have a quiet life. They're all connected in numerous ways that we don't know about."

"You think Shempire was lying to us?" I asked.

"I don't think so."

"How are the boys connected?" I asked.

Zane said, "I'm not sure yet. I have to think it over first."

"The life and times of the undercover detective. No wonder I like you."

"One of the first things I need to do is find Tab Fuller and Ashton Sniper."

"How are we going to find them?"

"We will. Never doubt me."

"I never said I did."

"I'm just giving you a heads up. Now, are you hungry?"

"Starving," I said with a heavy sigh.

"Good, because we're going to a wake and there'll be lots of food."

CHAPTER THIRTEEN
A TASTE OF DEATH

B en and Cort's aunt Penelope Yardage lived in a three-story on Gooserun Street. I walked in with Zane and was greeted by Penelope herself, a six-plus woman with fullback shoulders, too much lipstick, and a coal-black silk skirt just short of her knee. Kisses and hugs were shared at the doorstep. Penelope said, "Thank you for coming. Please, make yourselves at home. Food and drink are in the dining room."

Zane got a plate of fried chicken, potato salad, and freshly baked cornbread. I ate light, preferring a spinach salad with bacon dressing, a glass of lemonade, and a sliver of sliced cantaloupe. We ate in a part of the hallway between the kitchen and dining room, keeping two of Ben and Cort's cousins, Deidra and Kailey, company. Neither said anything regarding their cousins' murders. They discussed a makeup article in *Vogue*, Deidra's new girlfriend, and an upcoming play by a local lesbian playwright. The only thing we learned from the cousins was they had no association with the Pieney brothers and were only at the wake because of their pushy mother.

Once our lunches were finished, I followed Zane outside and we mingled with six male smokers. Zane discovered Tab Fuller sitting on the back steps of Aunt Penelope's home.

Twenty-something Tab smoked a cigar and sat hunched forward, resting his arms on his knees. He had an iced beverage between his legs. Obviously he was drunk; I could smell his six previous whiskey sours a mile away.

Zane didn't care that Tab was intoxicated. He stood at the bottom of the narrow white steps and said, "A gentleman like yourself looks like he could use a walk."

Tab looked up and asked, "Who are you?"

"Like yourself, a friend of Ben's."

"What do I need a walk for?"

Discreetly Zane flashed his badge, leaned forward, and said, "I'm with the Quill Village Police Department. I need to ask you a few questions, if you don't mind."

"Who's the squirt?" Tab asked, pointing the tip of his cigar in my direction.

I stepped up beside Zane and offered, "I'm also a friend of Ben's. Can you help us?"

Tab shook his head. He leaned his head between his open legs and vomited into his half-consumed drink.

Zane escorted me away from the disgusting scene, skirting around the house to his Durango.

During our walk along the side of the house, he pulled me beneath the canopy of a weeping willow tree. Hidden by the shade from the grieving guests, he began kissing me. I had just started to become excited when he pulled away and we heard Paula Pieney and her sister, Penelope, as they stopped outside the tree and began to whisper.

Huddled together, chest to chest, Zane and I listened.

Penelope: "Get rid of it. Throw it away. No one needs to know about that. The media will have a field day with a list like that. You can't expose Ben...I won't let you."

Paula: "I'll burn it after the guests leave. Ashes to ashes. Dust to dust. No one needs to know about it."

Penelope: "We can go into the garden right now and hide it in the sunflowers. We'll have it buried in no time."

Paula: "So someone can dig it up later? That's the most ridiculous thing you have ever said. Use your brain, sis."

Penelope: "You shouldn't have it. Someone will see it. The public doesn't need to know about Ben's interests."

Paula: "I don't have it. I'm not a fool. And I agree, no one needs to know what he was doing."

Penelope: "If you don't have it, where is it?"

Paula: "The spare bedroom, upstairs. The one I'm staying in. I'll burn it later. No one will find it."

The sisters moved away from outside the willow tree. Zane kissed me again. He said, "We can't leave yet."

I whispered exactly what he was thinking: "Off to the grieving mother's bedroom we go for clues."

"Indeed, Squirt."

"Don't call me that," I said, irritated.

❖

No one saw us go up the narrow stairs and enter the second floor of Penelope Yardage's home. On the right wall beside the staircase were family photographs. The sisters, Deidra and Kailey, were in a number of pictures, as Girl Scouts or at high school functions. There were several photos of Penelope and her three sisters at anniversaries, birthday parties, and summer vacations. Ben and Cort Pieney were in three of the photographs: Ben throwing a football during a championship football game; Ben wearing high heels at a young age; both Ben and Cort at a summer picnic along Lake Quill when they were young boys. A last photograph at the top of the stairs caught my interest. It looked like a digital print from maybe the summer before. There were seven shirtless men in the picture: Ben, Cort, Blaine, Jonas, Davido, Tab, and Ashton. Behind the bare-chested beauties was a wooden sign between two oaks. The sign read CAMP MINNOWTAH, LAKE SAMOY, NEW YORK—FOOTBALL DAY! I pointed the photograph out to Zane.

We looked into what must have been Penelope's private room. It was a Victorian paradise. There were ruffles galore, gold-plated mirrors, frilly doilies, and knickknacks of naked cherubs. The next bedroom on the right couldn't have been the one used by Ben and Cort's mother. There were no suitcases next to the bed and the drawers in the dresser were empty. A window opened to the backyard full of grieving guests. Even the closet was vacant.

I tugged on Zane's arm. "She's not staying in here. We have the wrong room."

Zane opened the door to the third bedroom.

Once inside, I immediately gasped at the sight of Paula's room and said, "Jesus, she's a little piggy."

Clothes were scattered across her unmade bed and the floor. Two empty beer cans sat on the dressing table near an eyelash curler, a hair dryer, and an assortment of makeup. Tissues looked as if they were flung about during a staged drama. A Nora Roberts paperback novel lay on the floor with its cover half ripped off.

"I would have never guessed she lived like this," Zane said.

I started pulling a night table's drawers open in search of the list. I found an empty box of Hostess doughnuts, two daily rags about Brad and Angelina, and a battered copy of Nicholas Sparks's *The Notebook*.

"Bingo," he said. "I think this is it."

He was near the bottom of the bed, looking under the sheet and scattered pillows. I turned around from the night table and watched him unzip a sheer cotton pillow covered in a butterfly slipcase. He pulled out a yellow piece of tablet paper and read it.

I moved up to his side and studied the troublesome list Paula and Penelope had mentioned.

Zane said, "You're breathing on my neck."

"Do you like it?"

"Don't get me started, lover boy."

The list contained an underlined heading, which read:

BEN = C

Beneath the heading were the names:

DAVIDO CHESWICK

TAB FULLER

ASHTON SNIPER

CHRIS MALONEY

ROBERT SAMSPIN

RUPERT CALLON

BYRON COPPENROD

CIVIC DAWSONDALE

VICTOR SKONESKI

HEATH DIXON

I asked, "What does the heading mean?"

Zane shrugged a shoulder and said, "Could be money owed to these guys. Could be a client drug list."

"Or prostitution," I suggested. "Maybe these guys are Ben's regulars."

"Or that."

"So how are we going to find out?"

"The old-fashioned way, Mr. Watson."

"You're so sexy when you're in detective mode, Zane," I said and planted a kiss on the side of his neck.

❖

Nina Bowel's office sort of resembled the spare bedroom that Paula Pieney was staying in at her sister's house. The windowless twelve-square-foot cube was cluttered with stacks of black binders and a mound of black-white notebooks filled with detective notes. There were two dirty coffee mugs and morsels of a stale doughnut on her desk. Next to her computer was a shelf displaying photographs of her two nephews. To the right of the nephews' photos was a black-and-white photograph of Carlita Roselli, who was Nina's attractive girlfriend. Carlita had majestic blue eyes and blond hair, perfect teeth, a thin nose, and perfect eyebrows.

When I picked up the photograph to admire the pretty woman up close, Nina barked, "Don't touch!" To the left of the Dell computer system was a bulletin board covered in morgue photographs of Ben and Cort Pieney. Close-ups detailed the brothers' butchered throats.

Nina clicked on a program called *QV Identification Query*. Zane and I watched her press a few buttons. She said to me, "This program will provide basic information regarding the persons on the list you found. The program is new and it's still in the process of being upgraded with information from local libraries, hospitals, colleges, and high schools. We've also gathered information from the county residential website to gain more details of our populace. If one of the persons on the list has committed a crime in the last ten years, their information should appear in our database."

I asked, "What kind of information will it provide?"

"The basics. Name. Age. Address. Telephone number. Highest level of education if we ask for it. And crimes." Nina punched the first name into the program and pressed Enter. What appeared surprised me:

DAVIDO CHESWICK. 35. (412) 555-7892
34 East Brason Street, Quill Village, NY 19834
History: August 13, 2003—Indecent Exposure

TAB FULLER. 23. (412) 555-9034
108 E. Walden Way, Quill Village, NY 19834
History: September 9, 2004—Public Intoxication
October 21, 2007—Public Intoxication
January 12, 2009—DUI

ASHTON SNIPER. 24. (412) 555-2653
12975 Saw Run Drive, Quill Village, NY 19834
History: March 3, 2006—Prostitution
October 15, 2007—Prostitution
February 17, 2008—Prostitution
May 9, 2010—Prostitution

CHRIS MALONEY. 20. (412) 555-9846
Quill College, Bessimer Hall, Floor 3, Room 312,
Quill Village, NY 19834
History: No results found

ROBERT SAMSPIN—No matches found

RUPERT CALLON. 19. (412) 555-9846
Quill College, Bessimer Hall, Floor 3, Room 312,
Quill Village, NY 19834
History: No results found

BYRON COPPENROD. 23. (412) 555-7826

Apartment 23, Highland Building, 217 Highland
Street, Quill Village, NY 19834
History: November 12, 2008—DUI
January 12, 2010—Indecent Exposure

CIVIC DAWSONDALE. 23. (412) 555-9820
219765 Jilling Avenue, Landing, NY 19835
History: February 19, 2009—Possession of drugs
April 4, 2010—Prostitution, Possession of drugs

VICTOR SKONESKI. 34. (412) 555-9820
Quill College, Lindon Hall. Floor 7, Room 722, Quill
Village, NY 19834
History: No results found

HEATH DIXON—No matches found

"Chris Maloney and Rupert Callon are roommates," I
observed.

"And Victor Dawsondale goes to the same college."

"All of these men are under thirty except for Davido
Cheswick and Victor Skoneski."

"You're thinking like a real detective now, Troy." She
winked at me and took a sip of Coke from a plastic bottle.

"Do you think this list is important?" I asked Nina.

"I'd say it's likely the Cutie Pie murderer is on that list."
Nina paused and asked, "What is your gut telling you?"

I didn't even have to think about it and said, "This is a list
of Ben Pieney's clients. They're all young guys who might
just be on Ben's booty call list."

"A prostitution ring?" Nina asked.

"Could be."

"What's your gut telling you, Troy?" She poked my

stomach with two fingers. "What's inside there? What's it saying?"

"I'm not sure," I said.

"Because you're a rookie. You need some more practice. Before you know it, your gut will be telling you everything. I promise."

❖

Zane and I walked out of Nina Bowel's office with our original list of Ben's clients and a printout of her supplied details from the *QV Identification Query*. While trotting to his Durango, he said, "Buddy, we have a lot of work ahead of us."

"Who are we going to talk to first?" I asked.

"You have your pick."

Sarcastically, I said, "This should be interesting. The highlight of my whole day."

CHAPTER FOURTEEN
FINDING MR. DIXON

We stopped at Delia's Danish Delights and I Googled Robert Samspin on my phone in the lounge area. Zane paid for two mocha lattes with light cream and gave me one. On the first Google hit I found Samspin's headshot (bright-white hair, blue eye shadow, black lipstick, pierced everything, a gap between his front teeth) and his address: 7564 Newberry Road, Landing. The second hit took me to his Facebook page, which featured a few lines of queer poetry. A few semi-naked pictures of himself drinking with his rowdy friends on a Friday night were also posted. The third hit took me to a site called *My Life, My Poetry, My Reflection.* Samspin had about twenty poems regarding gay men committing suicide, gay-bashing, and getting laid in the back of a VW on Hassle Street by an older man named Kazoo. We read some of Samspin's badly written poetry, decided we needed to kick our search up a notch, and left Delia's.

7564 Newberry Road was along Lake Quill in a low-rent district northwest of downtown. Zane parked in front of the dilapidated row house and climbed out of his Durango. Somewhere in the distance a woman screamed, "Here, baby! Here, girl!"

We made our way up to the front door.

Zane tapped on the broken screen door three times since there was no doorbell. A pit bull leaped at the door but was immediately pulled back by its leather collar by a heavyset white woman who held a pink-faced baby girl against her broad bosom and stared at us. She asked in a rather gruff manner, "What do you want?"

The woman smelled like she hadn't showered in days. Zane removed his sunglasses and unclipped his badge from his front pocket. He flashed the shield at the woman and said, "Detective Zane Ward of the Quill Village Police Department, ma'am. I was wondering if I could speak with Robert Samspin today."

The woman shook her head. Baby played with the woman's double chin, giggling. The pit bull showed its teeth, choked by its own collar and the woman's grip. "I don't talk to no police. You got da wrong house."

"Robert Samspin doesn't live here?" Zane asked.

"Not for the past tree years."

"Could you tell us where he lives?" I asked.

"What kind of shit is he in now?" She shifted the baby so she wouldn't fall to the dirty kitchen floor behind the screen.

Zane shook his head. "We just need a few questions answered about his friends."

"You're asking da wrong woman. I birfed him and I'm done with dat boy. A child should never take his mother's money. I will never forgive him for dat. He take from me. Broke my heart."

"Then who should we be asking?" I said.

"Daddy D takes care of him now."

"Who is Daddy D?" Zane asked.

The woman rocked her baby in her arms and said, "I don't know his name. He's a tough motherfucker who takes care of a few boys. Robby's one of dem. Daddy D is a social worker, I think. He runs a house for boys."

"What kind of care does he give the boys?"

"I don't know dat either."

"Do the boys do drug deals for him?"

"I told ya...I'm da wrong woman to ask. I don't know wud Robby does, and I don't really care. I'll care when he gives me back my seven thousand dollars he took from da cookie jar." Robby's mother started to become hostile.

Zane asked one final question. "Where can we find this Daddy D?"

"The Tai Chow Place on Marshall. Why, you going dere?"

"Maybe." Zane shrugged a shoulder.

She outstretched a finger and pointed it at us. "'Cause if you are, you tell dat boy I want my money. You tell him he broke me. You tell him I birfed him and it hurt. If he wants a mother...I want my fucking money. Do you hear me?"

We left.

❖

The Tai Chow Place at 72395 Marshall Street was a boarding house for street kids. Daddy D, we learned, was Walter "Daddy D" Dickinson, a thirty-year-old black male with, a medium-size build, mustache, and goatee. He sported bangle bracelets on both wrists, gold hoop earrings on his lobes, and a .45 caliber holstered against his right hip. At the front steps of the house, he asked in a flamboyant manner, "Who do you sexy boys want to see and why?"

"Robby," Zane said. "We have some business to discuss."

"What kind of business, darling?" Daddy D touched the weapon at his side and then waved a finger at us as if to say *Don't cross me. And don't think you can cross my boys. I don't want to have to fuck the two of you up.*

"Two guys were murdered and we need to ask him a few questions," I said.

"That football player and his brother?"

"Yes. Those two," Zane said.

"I'm sure sweet Robby has no connection to them. He knows so little about sports. Music is his gig."

"Can we speak with him?"

Daddy D stepped to the right and we walked inside.

The place seemed comfortable. Jazz played on the stereo. A few underage boys sat around a table and played poker with Q-tips instead of chips, all of them drinking cans of Pepsi. Two of the boys laughed. The house was clean and smelled pretty good for being in a rough part of the city.

Daddy D escorted us up a narrow flight of stairs. We made a left at the top and stopped at a closed door on the right-hand side of the hallway. A Keep Out sign hung on the door. D tapped three times on the door and called out Robby's name.

No answer.

D turned to us and said, "He likes music. Jazz. Big band. The Supremes. He's got good taste for someone so young. The boy always has headphones on and can't hear me knocking." He tapped three more times.

No answer.

"I'll have to crack the door to get his attention." D turned the knob and pushed the door open about four inches. Respectful of Robby's privacy, he didn't go inside. D turned to us again and said, "Now for the waiting game. He'll see the door open and he'll greet us. It may take a minute or ten, we'll see."

About a minute later Robby appeared at the door and D introduced us.

Robby was more attractive in person than his pictures online. He was minus the piercings, which made him look a little younger. His bright blue eyes flickered with concern and interest. With his innocent-looking face, he didn't look a day over sixteen.

"What do they want with me? I didn't do nothing wrong," Robby defended himself.

D said, "They want to ask you a few questions about the Pieney brothers."

The boy attempted to close the bedroom door in our faces when D stepped forward, preventing him from doing so. D said, "Don't be an ass, Robby. Make this easy on all of us. I'll protect you no matter what."

The trust between the boy and man was a sight to see. Apparently Daddy D was a positive role model in the boys' lives. Robby opened the door and allowed us to stand just inside the door and ask questions.

D said, "I'll leave the three of you alone."

"Stay," Robby requested.

D didn't move.

Zane didn't waste any time. "How old are you?"

"Eighteen. I'll be nineteen in December."

"There's a list with your name on it. The list is believed to be written by Ben Pieney. Why would your name be on it?"

"I don't know what you're talking about."

My partner pulled out a copy of the list and presented it to Robby. "How many of these guys do you know?"

Robby read over the list of names, shook his head, and said, "I don't know any of these people."

"Why don't I believe you?" Zane asked. He looked from the boy to Daddy D and back to the boy.

Daddy D said, "If he says he doesn't know any of them, he doesn't know."

"You carry drugs for these guys?" Zane asked.

"No."

"You sell drugs to them?"

"No. Daddy D wouldn't let me live here if I did that."

"He's right, Detective," Daddy D said. "I have a no-tolerance policy. All the boys know this when they first arrive."

"You have sex with these guys?"

"I don't and never have."

"No blow jobs? No backstreet fucks?"

"No...nothing like that."

"You know Heath Dixon?"

The boy looked up from the list and shook his head.

"You telling me the truth?"

Robby passed the list of names back to Zane. "Why would I lie?"

"Because your name is right there." Zane pointed to Robby's name on the list.

"You could have typed that list up on your office computer and added my name to it," Robby said with wide eyes and a straight face.

Zane didn't even flinch by the comment. "Will you let us in your room to look around?"

That was Daddy D's cue. He stepped between Robby and Zane. D said, "That won't be necessary. I think you've had enough of Robby's time."

Before we were escorted out of the Tai Chow Place, Zane made sure he got the last word in. He called over his right shoulder to the boy, "If you're hiding something, I'll find out what it is. You don't want me to come back here again. Trust me when I say that."

❖

Daddy D walked us to Zane's Durango. He pulled me next to him and whispered, "These boys have fucked-up lives. I'm here to help them when I can. They come from the worst homes. Parents who don't give a damn about them. Robby's mother is no different. The woman's on every drug imaginable and has no love for that boy."

Zane was already behind the wheel of the Durango.

I said, "Robby knows Heath Dixon."

Daddy D shut up and didn't move.

"So he was lying to Detective Ward?" I said to Daddy D.

Daddy D said, "Yes, but not out of harm. These boys see and hear things they don't want to see and hear. He didn't mean to lie, I'm sure. But he had to."

"Of course. How does Robby know Dixon?"

"They're boyfriends."

"For how long?"

"Six months...maybe longer."

"And where can we find Mr. Dixon?"

"You can't," Daddy D said.

"What do you mean I can't?"

D whispered, "Heath is dead. He went to visit his aunt Carmen in Los Angeles and never came back."

"How did he die? Drugs? Alcohol? Did someone pop him?"

D shook his head. "Nothing like that. He drowned in her swimming pool just two weeks ago."

"And that's why Robby lied. It's too fresh in his mind. The boy he loved drowned."

"Yes. Something like that," Daddy D said.

I looked up at the second-floor windows of the Tai Chow. I asked D, "How old was Heath Dixon?"

"Seventeen."

"Any guesses why he's on that list we showed Robby?"

"None."

"If you find out, you'll let me know, right?"

"Scout's honor," Daddy D said, and vanished inside the house.

❖

"Robby's lying and Daddy D's covering for him," Zane chewed on a stick of peppermint gum and drove us back to Precinct 29.

"Why do you say that?"

"It's my gut instinct. Robby's hiding something and D is covering for him. The guys in that house protect each other, which is no surprise."

"Your gut is telling you that?"

"My gut is very smart, Troy. I've figured out a lot of cases based on simple instinct." Zane made a right onto Sobner Street and continued to head north. My phone started to buzz inside my jeans. After three rings he asked, "You going to answer that?"

"It's trouble. Any fool knows that."

"That's more reason to answer it, then."

"Thanks, Mother Zane." It was my brother. I flipped the phone open and asked, "Cody, what's going on?"

"Liz dumped me." He sounded positively stunned, and broken. Cody was a pretty strong man, except for when it came to women and Mother's intrusions with them. Nine chances out of ten, he was about to fall into the depths of a depression and become lost and unbalanced again.

"Liz?"

"Yes, Liz...my girlfriend. She says she doesn't want to be involved with my family, which means Mother. She says she has her own family with baggage and doesn't need a second one."

Honestly, I wasn't floored. I did act surprised, though, and asked, "Liz said that?"

"Yes. Why do you seem so surprised?"

I cleared my throat and replied, "It's not that I'm surprised, Cody. It's...it's just that no one in their right mind battles Mother and comes across as being polite, friendly, or lovable."

"That's exactly what I told Liz. Before I knew it, she dumped me. It's over." His voice lingered and fell to hurt silence.

I looked over at Zane behind the driver's wheel. He was comfortably tucked in his own world of cops and criminals. I said, "I'll have a talk with Liz and see what I can do to save the two of you. Where is she?"

"The Cassidy Lounge."

"What the hell is she doing there? Doesn't she know that's a lesbian bar?"

"Yes, she knows. One of her friends owns the place. Liz wanted a drink and that's where she went. She says the place has the best jukebox in the city. It's loaded with Wham!, Madonna, and Prince singles."

I wanted to laugh, but didn't. Instead, I consoled my older brother the best way I knew. "I'll go talk to her right now." Poor Cody. If he didn't love Mother, he would have probably killed her.

"Right now?"

"Yes. I think it's best to get this out of the way and see the two of you move on with your lives, together."

"You're the best little brother in the world, Troy."

"I know," I said, disconnected our call, and informed Zane, "There's a little change in our plans. I need you to take me to the Cassidy Lounge."

Zane joked, "You looking for a sweet lesbian to cuddle with?"

"Yes," I said, grabbed his thigh with my left palm, and squeezed hard, "since you never put out."

❖

The Cassidy Lounge was on Peter Street in the lesbian district. Marla Cassidy had owned the establishment for the past thirty years and still enjoyed playing bartender. Unlike most gay bars, the place was clean and well lit and had more pool tables than patrons. Zane and I found Liz Bradbaum at the bar. She was working a bottle of light beer, humming "Everything She Wants" by Wham!, which was playing on the jukebox.

Zane went to play a game of pool while I sat next to Liz. Marla asked what I wanted to drink, and I ordered a vodka tonic, something strong to get me through my ordeal with Cody's ex-girlfriend. Immediately, I gained Liz's attention with, "Minnie is a raving lunatic bitch."

She took a drink of her beer and turned to me. "That's not very nice to say about your own mother."

Honestly, I loved to bad-talk Mother. Any chance I could get, she turned into my victim. The woman had it coming, of course, since she had emotionally abused both of us boys since we were babies.

"It's the truth. Minnie is a controlling oppressor who needs to mind her own business. She also needs to start being nice to people, especially those friends and significant others that her two sons bring home to meet her."

Liz smiled. "You're making me feel better."

"You've broken my brother's heart. I haven't seen him this way since Minnie caught him masturbating at age twelve."

"I didn't mean to. It's just…it's just…"

"Mother Minnie Murdock is a monster who has always liked to eat Cody's girlfriends as appetizers, Liz. I like to call her repugnant and unholy. Something from hell. Sometimes I would like to call Father Trotten down at St. Mary's to perform an exorcism on her."

She chuckled. "But that's your mother," she said.

"It doesn't matter." I patted her right arm and said, "You are now a secret member of Minnie rebels. We love and despise the woman at the same time. We say the worst things about her and still find a tiny place in our hearts to love and care for the woman. And never do we share our true feelings with her regarding her villainous behavior. Now, welcome to our association." I reached for her hand and shook it.

"I like you," Liz said, shaking my hand and smiling. "Cody promised me you would be my BFF."

"You have to be with my brother. He's very into you. You make him happy and whole. The man is nothing without you. Never have I gotten involved in his life regarding women… but you're perfect for this family, Liz. Trust me, you're worth this talk."

"I know that." She sighed heavily and said, "I've made a mess out of this. Shame on me for overreacting."

"Now, now." I patted her arm again. "Don't demean yourself. Minnie would like that too much. I suggest you call Cody and work this out with him."

"If he'll have me."

"He wants nothing more," I insisted.

Liz took another sip of her beer and "Careless Whisper" started playing on the jukebox. Following her sip, she asked, "Can I hug you for helping me?"

I smiled and cheerily said, "A kiss on the cheek will be nice, too."

CHAPTER FIFTEEN
SKINNY-DIPPING

A t approximately ten fifteen that evening, Nina informed Zane that Rupert Callon was a BB.

Zane and I were in his Durango and cruised down Roughton Street on the north side of the city. We had just finished a rather romantic dinner at an Italian place called Nino's. He played footsie with me under the table, flirted with me, and picked up the tab. Now it was all business. "What's a BB?" He had his cell on speakerphone.

"A bottom boy. Rupert likes a lot of action in his back door."

"No shit?"

I chuckled in the passenger seat. I didn't know where we were heading and left it up to Zane. Maybe we were going out dancing at Pablo's Club. Or maybe he was escorting me back to his house where he would rip my clothes off and have his hungry way with me.

"It's something his family is not very proud of," Nina said. "The mafia family is loaded, a well-known name in politics."

He winked at me, blew me a kiss, and said, "I definitely have an agenda with the guy."

Nina asked, "You going to drill him, Zane?"

"You bet. Let's see what he has to share."

Nina said to be careful and be on our best behavior.

Zane responded, "I'm never bad, darling...you know that."

"You're never good, either. And don't call me darling," was Nina's response before she hung up.

Zane drove through a set of wrought-iron gates toward the Quill River and steered us into Quill Village Park, which was quiet and serene. Although the park was exceptionally enchanting with its fairy-tale ambience, dim golden lights, and cobblestone walkways, it was a playground for crime. Bottom line: if you didn't want trouble, you stayed out of the park at night.

I asked, "How do you think Rupert is connected to the Pieney murders?"

"Most likely drugs. The guy is hooked. Nina says he's a trafficker."

"He a user?"

"What trafficker isn't a user?"

"Good point. Do you think Pieney was a user?"

"Which one?" he asked.

"Both."

"Yes for Cort. Maybe for Ben. I guess we'll find that out from Callon."

❖

Rupert Callon's father ran thirty percent of the city's crime.

We met Rupert near the Quill. It was now ten thirty and the humidity had thickened, leaving us sticky with ripe perspiration. The night sky was clear with an arrangement of glittery stars. Across the Quill River, the QV Quails brought the twelve thousand baseball fans in the stadium to an excited roar.

Rupert arrived at the statue of Admiral Wayne Erroneous with two bulky African American cohorts, each of whom was bigger than Zane and me put together. Rupert smoked a cigar, looked quite relaxed actually, and asked me in his deep voice, "What do you want?"

Zane stepped in front of me and said, "You know about Ben Pieney's list?"

"The quarterback?"

"The murdered quarterback."

"What list?" Rupert smiled.

Zane presented a copy of our found list to him. "Your name is number six. Any idea why you're on it?"

"Any reason why I'm not number one?"

"I'll move you to the number one position if you tell me why you're on the list."

Rupert read the ten names again and confessed, "I don't want to be on this fucking list." He passed the sheet of paper back to Zane and shook his head.

"Why not?" I stepped out from behind Zane. "The least you can do is give us that much."

Zane passed the list to me; I folded it and tucked it away in my jeans.

"I'm not telling you two shit," Rupert replied. "You're vice. You think I'm that stupid not to know which side you're on?"

Zane asked, "How many of those guys on the list do you know?"

"All of them."

"Do they work for you?"

"No."

"Do you work for them?"

"What the fuck kind of question is that? Of course I don't."

"You know why they're connected to Ben Pieney?"

"Maybe."

"You want to tell me how?"

"Not really."

"You kill Ben and his brother?"

"Do I look like I killed the fag and his brother?"

Zane shook his head and said, "I didn't think it would hurt to ask, though."

"Don't ask stupid fucking questions." Rupert looked over his right shoulder at his hulking twosome. He looked back at us and said, "I was buddies with Ben. There's no way I could have killed him. I liked him too much."

"What kind of buddies?" Zane asked.

"That's none of your fucking business, pal." Rupert's tone turned even more aggressive. Obviously, he was losing his patience with us. The two bodyguards stepped forward and removed pistols from their belts. Both weapons were aimed at Zane and me.

Rupert shifted his view from us to his two chums and snapped, "No game! They're cops. Don't overreact. Put the shit away. You don't kill pigs."

The henchmen stepped a foot back. Both seemed disgruntled they couldn't blow us away.

Rupert calmed down and said to Zane, "Pieney liked to have fun. I was the guy he sometimes called to arrange that fun."

"Sex or drugs?" Zane asked.

"Yes. Whatever and whenever. Pieney liked to party. He was wild. The fearless quarterback. I arranged some parties for him."

"He pay you to do that?"

"Sometimes. Other times, it was on the house."

"And the guys on the list showed up for his parties?"

"Maybe. It depended whether Pieney wanted them there or not. Like I said, whatever and whenever. He felt comfortable having an entourage. He was important and knew it. Without his entourage of guys he was nothing. Those were the men who did things for him. The movers and shakers. His network."

"And you were part of his entourage?"

Rupert nodded and shared another smile. "Just like the other nine guys on your list."

❖

The more I learned about Ben Pieney off the football field, the more I disliked the man. So Pieney had an entourage, men he had parties and fun with, cohorts to do drugs with, ten sexy guys to fuck around with and…

"I believe Rupert. What about you, Troy?" Zane asked. We walked away from the bronze statue, returning to the Durango.

"I don't know who or what to believe. Some of it sounds believable. I'm sure most of it is bullshit, though." I was exhausted and stressed and just wanted to cool off.

He tried to soothe my frustration and said, "We're getting closer to the end, I can feel it. Something tells me this list of Ben's entourage will solve both murders for us."

"I feel like we're beating our heads against the wall."

"That's what it's always feels like. Hang in there with me. Something's going to break, and soon. I've done this many times and…Are you listening to me?"

I wasn't. The heat had finally bitch-slapped me. I was exhausted and uncomfortably sweaty. "I'm sorry. It's really sticky and hot out."

He rubbed a palm over my back. "Hang in there. I'm overworking you."

Back at his Durango, I climbed into the passenger seat again and sighed heavily. "I'm fucking miserable and need a swim. You game?"

"Does Mother Minnie have a pool?" Zane dripped with sweat. Beads of perspiration ran down and over his forehead, cheeks, and neck. He kicked on the air conditioner as high as it would go, but it didn't seem to help.

"No, but my aunt Felicity does. She's out of town and I have a spare key."

"Where's this special aunt live?"

"Faulkner."

"Twenty minutes isn't far."

"You're game, then?"

"You had me with that adorable sigh, guy. Of course I'm in."

❖

Aunt Felicity was my father's sister and on a mission to find her brother. Loaded by her four ex-husbands, my fifty-nine-year-old aunt spent thousands on her investigation. She returned every three months from her travels and updated all of us on her worthless findings. Aunt Felicity had not found my father but was still on the search, and left her house empty for me to use, anytime I desired. Currently she was somewhere in the west with her Buick, playing detective and learning new clues about my father's strange vanishing.

I stood by the edge of Aunt Felicity's Olympic-size pool: outside and secluded by ivy-covered wrought-iron fences, lit a pastel blue, with granite decking and two diving boards. I watched Zane strip out of his clothes.

I couldn't stop admiring him in the buff: taut shoulders, perfectly lined stomach, perky nipples, and Herculean biceps. Before he performed a flawless dive into that water underworld, he gleamed with a devilish smile and promised, "Meet me at the bottom and I'll rock your world."

Because his dive was graceful and executed with utter precision, there was next to no splash. He swam to the deep end of the pool, touched bottom, and waited there for me.

Although I wanted to take a dive in the glistening pool, my attention was drawn to my left. Summertime branches cracked in the nearby woods beyond the wrought-iron gate that led in and out of the pool area. Nervously, I called, "Who's there?" Again, I called out to the fence and dark woods, "Who are you? What do you want?"

To my utter surprise, Luanne Ringle stepped into the pool area, spotlighted by silver-white moonbeams. She wore evening-white capris, a skimpy halter top, and a sleek pair of woven sandals. She clutched a smallish purse under right arm. Embarrassed by my birthday suit, she said, "I didn't mean to interrupt."

I covered up my goods with both hands. What was going on? Did Luanne follow us to Aunt Felicity's? Were we being stalked? How long was she hiding in the woods beyond the protective fence? How much of my conversation with Zane did she hear? How did she find us, and why?

Zane could not hold his breath at the bottom of the pool any longer and surfaced in the hip-deep water. He shook water from his head like a dog. "What the fuck are you doing here, Luanne?"

Luanne ignored the question. "I have a bit of information that can maybe help you, Troy." She reached out and grasped my right wrist.

"What kind of help?"

She looked at me and said, "I might know who killed the Pieney brothers."

"Tell me who did it," I said. "This better be good. Don't waste my time."

"I'll make you a deal, Troy."

"Do you intend to blackmail me?" I found my pile of clothes, pulled out my boxers, and slipped them on.

She watched me pull the cotton up to my navel. "It's not blackmail. I call it a safety net."

"Call it whatever you want, it's still blackmail." Luanne's untimely arrival had ruined my alone time with Zane and a way to cool off from the sticky and heated evening.

Zane climbed out of the pool and headed for his clothes.

Luanne said, "Listen to me. I'll tell you who killed the brothers if you tell me when Ivan contacts you."

I rolled my eyes, slipped a T-shirt over my head, and said, "Deal. Now, tell me what you know."

She opened her purse and pulled out a four-by-six black-and-white photograph, which she passed to me. "Take a look at this."

I took in the photograph. The twenty-something guy was heartbreakingly pretty with a flawless complexion, semi-slanted eyes, thick onyx-colored hair, and a boy-next-door smile. He didn't look a day out of college and resembled something sweet and charming.

"Who is this?" I asked.

"You tell me who it is," she challenged.

I showed the picture to Zane, now fully dressed at my side. He gave the head shot a quick glance and said, "I never saw him before. Who is it?"

"He worked for Ben Pieney."

Zane and I shared a confused look.

He gave the photograph another glance and asked, "What do you mean by that, Luanne?"

I took the photograph from him and passed it back to

Luanne. She said, "His name is Byron Copenrod. He was Ben's houseboy for the past two years."

Zane said, "He's number seven on the list."

"What list?"

"The none of your fucking business list," he said. He yanked the photo of Byron from Luanne's fingers. "I'll need this. When I'm done with it, you'll get it back from me."

She asked me, "What about Ivan? Are you going to help me or not?"

I nodded.

"Where does Copenrod live?" Zane asked.

"124 Whitman Circle. He lives with his uncle or something like that."

"How'd you find this out?"

"That's none of your fucking business, pal." Luanne zoomed away through the wrought-iron gate and into the woods.

Two events transpired during the lightning-speed drive to 124 Whitman Circle to find Byron Copenrod. The first was rather simple. Zane said, "Promise me we'll swim together at your aunt's pool."

I chuckled in the Durango's passenger seat. "I can arrange that. Sorry about the interruption."

"That woman's crazy. She needs to be put away. She's going to hurt herself one of these days."

"Do you think she's bullshitting us?"

"My gut says she's not."

"You always trust corndogs?" I put my head back for a short rest and closed my eyes.

Zane sniggered. "Not always. It's the wieners I trust. I like them better."

"That's pretty noble, and hot. Something told me you were a wiener kind of guy."

"Noble and charming, that's me."

The second event during the drive was a text message from my brother. I flipped my Nextel open and read: MOTHER IS AT IT AGAIN.

I typed in: *Wut?*

THREATENED ELIZABETH AGAIN.

How?

BARBED WIRE. LIKE THE QV KILLER.

OMG she didn't?

DID.

Why?

MOTHER'S AFRAID SHE WILL HURT ME.

Why?

OVERPROTECTIVE!!!

Nuf said. Understood. I will handle Mother.

TY.

Welcome.

KEEP ME POSTED.

I typed in *Will do*. Then I called Mother's cell. Her voicemail picked up but I didn't leave a message. I then called her house and she picked up after the second ring. Following her hello, I barked, "Mother, you cannot go postal on Elizabeth and threaten her life!"

"Who?"

"Mother! Listen to me! Apologize to that woman! She's important to Cody and—"

She hung up on me. I redialed her number and listened to a busy signal. I pressed the End button on my Nextel, redialed a second time, and heard another busy signal. "Fuck!" I barked, which startled Zane, causing him to swerve into oncoming traffic.

Both of us hollered as a Mack truck thundered toward us.

Zane spun the wheel to the right and zoomed back into our lane, left out a sigh of relief, and confessed, "I think I just went in my pants."

"Great!" I said. "You shit yourself and my family's going to end up on Dr. Phil!"

CHAPTER SIXTEEN
LIFE IMITATES ART

The Tudor-style home at 124 Whitman Circle was owned by a Mr. Timothy Mantra, a retired photographer for *The Daily Quill*; he was also Byron Copenrod's uncle. The entire property was trimmed to perfection. There was no car in the narrow drive. When Zane peered through a crescent-shaped garage window with a penlight, he didn't see a vehicle parked inside. Coming up empty-handed, he said, "No luck. There's no one here."

"The boy could be sleeping inside. We need to check it out."

"If no one lets us inside that's considered breaking and entering."

I ignored him and made my way up to the front door. I tried the brass doorbell, listened to a Mozart piece play inside the house, and waited for Mr. Mantra or boy wonder to open the door.

Zane knocked on the front door three times, listened for a response, didn't receive one, tugged on my right arm, and said, "No answer. That means we're leaving."

I pulled free from him, tried the waist-high brass knob on the front door, and found that it was miraculously open. "It looks like we're welcome. So much for leaving with your tail between your legs, pal."

He was adamant about not trespassing, shook his head in a rather dogged and persistent manner, and said, "I could lose my badge if I go in there. You wouldn't want that to happen to the guy you have a crush on, right?"

"Good. I completely understand. You can stay out here while I look for clues. Just make sure you don't call the police on me."

He reached for my shoulder. He asked, "What kind of clues are you looking for?"

"Barbed wire and yellow pins. The necessary tools to commit murder, of course."

"What makes you think you'll find them here?"

"Look, Mr. Pessimistic, it's not going to hurt. If memory serves me right, you got me into this. I'm only trying to help the best way I know how. Besides, we have to find Byron and determine if he's innocent or a bloodthirsty killer."

Saved by the hum of his cell! He reached into his front pocket and retrieved the device. "Nina, what's going on?"

There was no point in standing at the front door of 124 Whitman Circle, so I made my way inside.

❖

Timothy Mantra's living quarters were not at all what I had expected. Eleven human-size sculptures in bright-white concrete decorated the foyer and attached sitting room. The art pieces were naked with swollen chests, buttocks, and cocks, their torsos wrapped with razor-sharp barbed wire. The wire, painted blood red, also wrapped around their narrow ankles, wrists, and smooth throats, and splotches of the red paint accented pectoral muscles and genitals. I called to Zane, still by the front door, "Buddy, you'd better get your ass in here and take a look at this! You're not going to believe what's in here!'"

He walked into the room and stood next to me. "What is this freak show?"

"Looks like we found where the barbed wire came from in the Pieney murders."

Zane walked from one statue to the next, studying each with a bemused look, and said, "I dated a dude who looked similar to these guys."

"I didn't know you were into bondage and albinos. Lady Gaga would love these guys."

He laughed and said, "Our romance lasted a whole ten seconds."

"Did he dump you or did you dump him?"

"I dumped him. The guy was a louse. All he wanted was sex. Twenty-four-seven."

"I'm surprised by that, Zane. I thought you were into red paint and barbed wire wrapped around your balls."

"Not in this lifetime, chap. Rough is not really up my alley. I thought you knew that."

"I do," I joked. I touched one of the statues, which felt like a smooth grade of cold sandpaper. My fingers found a barb on the faux human chest and felt its sharp points. I said, "The wire is real. No fakes here."

"We need to get it checked out. I have to call Nina and get a warrant so—"

Something or someone snorted upstairs. I looked at him and he looked at me. I pointed to the oak stairs that spiraled to Timothy Mantra's second floor. Another sound; this time it was more of a grunt than a pig's snort. Zane carefully moved around two statues, found himself in front of me, and silently pulled me with him up the fifteen steps.

The stairs creaked under our weight. My sidekick had his

9mm gripped with both hands, and his back slid against the bare wall, painted a blaring white. We heard another muffled cry. The voice sounded strangled, lost, parched, and somewhat distant. At the top of the stairs to our left in the dim T-shaped hallway, we saw a room without a door. To our right were two doors, one open and one closed. I saw a teal-colored tile wall inside the open room, and...

A second muffled cry came from behind the closed door to our right. Zane leaned into me; his shoulder pressed lightly against my shoulder. He brushed his lips to my left ear and whispered, "Follow me, heartbreaker. I'll cover you."

He stepped in front of the door and I stood behind his sexy and firm body. Another grunt was heard behind the door. Zane quickly peered over his left shoulder to see if we were being followed by a shooter or bad guy. The hallway was empty.

I stood on his right and we listened to more grunts behind the door.

Timothy Mantra's spare bedroom was locked from the inside. Zane kicked the door in with his right foot. The plane of wood instantly flew open, breaking one hinge. On guard, he immediately extended his right arm and pointed the 9mm into the room. Whoever was in the spare room stopped my sidekick in his tracks and left him awestruck. I heard him swear, with deep concern in his voice, "Jesus Christ...he's alive."

❖

Byron Copenrod, number seven on the list Zane and I had discovered, was completely naked and bound in four strands of red-painted barbed wire. He was pinned to a high-back reading chair, gagged with a white sock, and unable to move. Barbed wire was wrapped around his genitals, his torso in two places, and around his neck. Tears shone in the boy's eyes as we entered the room. Zane was on his cell, calling the station for backup as I started to play hero and helped Byron out.

After removing the white sock from the young man's mouth, I attempted—and failed miserably, mind you—to unwind the barbed wire from around his neck.

The room was basic: a single American Tourister suitcase, open at the bottom of a full-size bed with Byron's personal belongings inside; two country landscape paintings by an amateur artist on the wall behind the bed; a maple dresser with mirror. The room looked clean and unlived in.

Byron Copenrod was still captive in the chair. The twenty-three-year-old had deep purplish-blue eyes, a muscled torso, and brownish-red curly hair, as well as chiseled shoulders and a corded neck. My stare traveled down over his rippled chest to his hairless navel.

Zane knelt in front of the young man and asked, "What the fuck happened in here?"

Byron looked weak and pallid. Thick lines of perspiration ran down his brow.

"Can you help us out, buddy?"

Byron gargled a few unintelligible words and began to blink.

Zane, already removing the barbed wire from the boy's torso, said, "Slowly. Speak slowly and we can help each other. No one's going to hurt you now."

"Here...tried to kill me...scared him away."

I was right beside Zane and Byron, listening. I couldn't make out what the victim was saying.

"Slower...and calm down," Zane soothed. "You're okay. More help is on the way. What do you mean by here?"

"He was here," Byron said, his voice almost inaudible. "He tried to kill me. You scared him away."

"Who did we scare away?" Zane asked.

Byron began to cry. His pale cheeks started to color as he stated, "I don't know who it was. He was wearing a black mask and black gloves. He made me strip out of my clothes and fold them in a pile. He said if I cooperated with him I wouldn't die. Then he tied me to this chair with my uncle's barbed wire."

"How do you know it was a man?" I asked.

"I just do. He had a big frame and hands."

Zane was unable to loosen the barbed wire from Byron's torso, needing a pair of heavy-duty wire cutters for the job. He stood and asked, "Where did the guy go who did this to you?"

"He went out the window. There's a small ledge out there with latticework."

Zane moved to the window. "What else did he say to you?"

"Nothing. Quiet like a mouse."

"You think he was going to kill you?"

"Yes. There was no doubt in my mind. The guy is totally fucked up."

"Did you know him? Can you tell us what he looked like?"

"No and no," Byron said. He let out a heavy sigh. "Aren't you going to get me out of this wire?"

I saw blood on Byron's chest and around his private parts. The barbed wire's teeth sank into his flesh. I whispered to him, "Medics are on their way. You'll be in good hands from here out."

Zane walked toward us.

"Is Nina on her way?" I asked.

"Did your uncle do this to you?" Zane asked, standing over the boy and me.

"I know his art pieces suggest he's a psycho, but Uncle

Tim would never hurt me." The boy was in pain. He squinted and ground his teeth, fending off bolts of sting from the strands of wire that continued to dig into his flesh.

I asked, "Do you know an Ashton Sniper, Byron?" Again, I picked a random name from the list of ten.

"I don't."

"Heath Dixon?"

"No."

"Rupert Callon?"

"Never heard of him. What's this all about, anyway?"

"I'll tell you in a little while. How about a Davido Cheswick or Jonas Smith?"

"Neither," the boy mumbled, tears flowing down his cheeks and into his mouth.

Zane said, "The fucker's lying. You can see it in his eyes. I've seen that look many times before."

"I'm not hiding anything...honestly."

Zane pulled on a latex glove, moved to the windowsill to look for any clues, and was back in front of the boy within just a few seconds. He looked spooked. "I believe you...really, I do."

"What's up, Zane? What's going on?" I asked.

He held up a yellow pin that said *Cutie Pie Must Die!* "I found this on the windowsill. Our killer was here. The boy's telling the truth. This place now officially belongs to the QVPD."

❖

A chopper circled overhead as Nina arrived at the crime scene. A team of cops hovered around Byron and carefully removed the four strings of barbed wire from his flesh. Nina had Zane place the killer's *Cutie Pie Must Die!* pin in a plastic baggie. Byron was removed from the room, sobbing and still in shock. He would be shipped to QV Hospital for a thorough exam and then questioned.

Zane said to Nina, "Send the barbed wire down to forensics with the pin. We need to see if it's a match with the barbed wire used on the Pieney brothers. Get a sample of the blood by the chair. Take as many prints as your team can of the entire room. Let's rock and roll with this, since the killer is at large. We have very little time to find him."

Nina was about to get to work when Zane leaned into her and calmly said, "Someone needs to talk to the boy, too. We need to find out how he's connected to the Pieney brothers and why his name is on the list. I want to be the first to hear the answers."

"Yes, sir," Nina said.

He directed his attention my way. "I have to get you out of here, Troy. No offense, but you're in the way."

Zane gave my elbow a little squeeze for comfort. He escorted me past a group of QVPD workers, down the stairs, out the front door, and back to his Durango. Gently, he touched my cheek with his lips and questioned, "You okay after all that?"

"I'm good. I could handle it."

"You're not sick to your stomach?"

"I've seen worse. Thanks for caring, though."

He opened the Durango's passenger door for me and I climbed inside. Before I knew it, we were heading east, which prompted me to ask, "Where are we going?"

"You're going home. I have an appointment to go to."

I wanted to ask who he was going to visit/question, but decided to mind my own business.

I was dropped off at the salon's front door. He leaned over the seat and kissed me a farewell. Following his melting kiss, he said, "I'll call you later."

"Thanks for all the danger today."

He smirked. "It comes with the package."

Before exiting the Durango, I said, "To tell you the truth, I can live without the danger. I just need your package."

"Stop your craziness. I'm going to blush."

"Don't get killed, Mr. Detective."

"Not a chance, guy. I like you too much for that to happen."

I watched his Durango drive away. Part of me secretly missed him already. The sane side of me said never to fall in like again with a man, certainly not after Ivan Reed. Better to stay single, uncommitted, and have the time of my life at boy-infested parties with loads of beer and drugs. Petty drama always seemed to ensue in my life when I was attached to a man. I was happy being single and didn't need a man to make things better; Zane sort of fell into that understanding, I guessed. In truth, though, I couldn't help the tingles inside my stomach. He was hazardous for me and had already placed me in numerous deathly situations. Our chemistry was strong, though, and honest. I strangely felt safe with him. I felt cared for when he was careless. I felt needed when he was…

No way. I wasn't going to fall in like with him, I warned myself, because he was statistically, physically, and emotionally hazardous. There was no way I could connect to another man like that, no matter how charming, precarious, and careless he was. My life at that moment was above average and looked better by each passing day; shame on me for thinking about messing the process up with him in the mix of things.

❖

The next morning, I was in the salon figuring out the books when Umberto pulled me off to the side and said, "Some hot, big number of a stud stopped here looking for you."

"Who was it?"

"I can't remember, sister. He left his card for you, which is right here. I don't want to be a nosy nib, Troy, but he was working his bod like no tomorrow. The guy was Russian and steamy to the core. Sexy-creamy good stuff, if you know what I mean."

Umberto left to use the bathroom. His departure prompted me to review the business card. I picked it up and read:

VICTOR SKONESKI
PERSONAL CONSULTANT

Underneath the name and title were Victor's cell number and a personal note to me in red ink:

I know you're looking for me. Call me. V.S.

CHAPTER SEVENTEEN
THE UNDERGROUND MAN CLUB

B efore I could call Victor, Mother Minnie showed up at the shop with one of her best friends, Prissy Palentine, who demanded a fresh and stylish cut from Umberto. Mother pulled me into my office, closed and locked the door behind us, and demanded, "I need something strong to drink. What do you have?"

Umberto kept a very potent bottle of gin in one of the desk drawers for such occasions. I pulled the blue bottle out.

Mother removed a rocks glass from her gold sequin shoulder bag and placed it on the corner of the desk. She met my eyes and said, "One must always be prepared for a bad day, Troy. Now, stop looking at me like that and pour me a drink. I don't want to hear your judgments. I just want two fingers' worth without ice."

I poured her the suggested two fingers of alcohol. "Why are you having a bad day?"

She scooped up the gin and emptied half of its contents in a matter of seconds. "Cody has placed me into a very sticky situation. He's given me an ultimatum. I was told to start getting along with Elizabeth or I will lose a son. How ridiculous is that? Can you believe he had the balls to do this to me?"

Actually, I could, but wasn't ballsy enough to tell Minnie that. Cody was hardcore sometimes, particularly regarding the women he dated throughout the years. Bottom line, he got what he wanted and he considered his relationship with Elizabeth serious. By the sounds of it, nothing was going to stand in the way of him and Elizabeth, including Mother.

Mother finished off her gin and demanded more; no surprise there. I thought about discussing with her the amount of gin she took down, but didn't; better to stay the good son while Cody was in her psychotic spotlight. "Take another drink. You need it. This news is shocking."

Mother blinked, nodded, and began to drink her second two fingers. After her first swallow, she shared, "It is shocking news, isn't it? Cody won't discuss the issue with me. He said our discussion is over. Can you believe that, Troy? I imagine he is ready to disown me next. He said I have to resolve this matter on my own and doesn't want to speak to me until I do."

"How do you feel about that, Mother?" I fingered Victor Skoneski's business card and wanted to kick Mother out of my office so I could contact Victor. Instead, I listened to her jabber.

"There's nothing to resolve. Liz has got to go. We don't get along."

"Why don't you like her? She's seems sane, nice, and generous. The woman has a career. She isn't bitchy or filthy."

"She's just not right for Cody. A mother knows these things. You don't understand."

"Is any woman right for Cody?" I asked, perturbed. "Take that into consideration. Your expectations for your two sons exceeds our limits. We will never be perfect for you, nor will our chosen partners." Okay, so I kind of blew it with keeping my composure. She was really starting to get under my skin.

"That's ridiculous! Of course there's a woman in the world for Cody. Think outside of the box, Troy."

"Why isn't Elizabeth that woman?"

Silence. She took another sip of Umberto's imported gin. She placed the back of her left hand against her forehead and said, "I'm not feeling well, baby. I need to sit down. I think I have a high temperature. Maybe the bird flu is setting in."

I knew she only called me baby when she was in desperate need of attention.

I watched her sit down in one of the office chairs and lean her head against the olive-white-black wall. She let out a Golden Globe–worthy sigh, took another sip of gin, and said, "I'm doomed to not being loved."

I rolled my eyes. "You need to think about how to make this better with your son and his girlfriend."

"Me? What about your brother? He's in the wrong. The man just can't bring any woman into my life and expect me to like her. I have conditions and standards. He needs to obey my wishes."

Leave it to Mother to say something like that. I bit my upper lip. Once I gathered my composure, I said, "Elizabeth is not just anyone. She loves Cody. And I personally know that Cody feels something strong for the woman. You need to face this, Mother. You're the one with the problem."

"I can't. I won't. I don't have any problems." She took another drink of gin and shook her head in a vehement manner.

"You should give Elizabeth a chance. That's not fair to your son. And that's not fair to you. As I said before, think about it."

She released another sigh and said, "I won't get along with her. It's against my better judgment. The woman is nothing like me, and I refuse to have her in our family."

Dammit! My cell phone rang. I looked down at the number

and saw that it was Zane. Quickly, I informed Minnie, "Excuse me, but this is very important. I really have to take it."

While I walked out of the office, I heard Mother say, "That's right, Troy, leave me. Treat my dilemma as nothing. I understand. I completely understand. Everyone else is important in your life except for me."

I closed the office door behind me and headed for the unisex bathroom and privacy.

❖

Zane declared, "The barbed wire found at 124 Whitman Circle does not match the barbed wire at the Pieney crime scenes."

"Nina doesn't waste any time, does she?"

"That's why she works for me. She's the best, and knows her shit. The woman knows how to do her job and no one can tell me different. The chair and floor have no fingerprints on them. There were no fingerprints on the windowsill or barbed wire, either. Whoever is doing this is clean about it."

"Any hair follicles?" I asked.

"Nada. Not a one."

"What about the pin? Does it match the other two? No blood on it? No fingerprints? Any luck yet?"

"Nina won't know until tomorrow."

"I'll be patient."

"That's a good boy. You do that, Detective Troy."

Another caller beeped into my phone. I told Zane, "Gotta run. My brother's trying to reach me. I'll talk to you soon."

He clicked off with: "Adios, compadre. Until later."

I pressed the Send button on my cellular and asked Cody, "What's going on?"

"Tell me Mother's not with you flapping her gums."

"She's here."

"Shit! The woman is driving me mad, Troy. How can I get through to her that Elizabeth is not a monster?"

"I'm working on that. Right now, our mother is having a gin date, perhaps thinking about her wrongdoings regarding you and Liz."

"Is she drunk?" he asked.

"Getting there."

He shared a devious laugh and said, "Brothers before mothers, right?"

"I only want you to be happy, and for Mother to accept your choices. Elizabeth brings out the best in you. I'd like to see her as an addition to this family. The woman has a lot to offer."

"I appreciate everything you're doing. Keep me posted about Mother."

"I'll do that," I said, and ended our communication with a simple good-bye.

❖

Ivan Reed must have entered the unisex bathroom behind me.

"Did Umberto tell you I was in here?"

"No. I found your mother in your office. She told me your whereabouts."

"Leave it to her."

"She's quite toasted and talking about someone named Lizard."

"Ivan. Just tell me what you're doing here."

"Luanne is threatening to take her life."

I wondered when Ivan's problems with Luanne became

my problems. How did I let that happen? What frame of mind was I in for getting involved with him again? Hadn't our lives disconnected in the past year? Shame on me for being so stupid and selfless, but come on…he was no different than Mother, in my opinion; both were sending me into a moat of insanity because of their drama.

He zipped up and went to the sink to wash his hands.

I asked, "How am I part of this?"

He soaped up his hands and rinsed. "You need to talk to Luanne for me."

"And what am I going to say to her?" Honestly, enough was enough. She was a pain in the ass, and Ivan was getting there. "No. Before you answer that…just listen to me. I can't help you, Ivan. It's not a battle I feel comfortable fighting for you. You're going to have to accomplish this on your own. You broke my heart to get with Luanne, if you remember."

He dried his hands and asked, "I thought you loved me?"

I nodded. "At one time I did. My feelings are not like that now. Things have changed between us. We're no longer boyfriends. Our lives are very different now. It is what it is, and you're going to have to realize that."

He caught me totally off guard with his next statement. "I understand. It's all crystal clear to me, pal."

I didn't know what to do or say. I just stood there.

Ivan started to cry. He had turned away from me and faced the wall.…

What was a little consoling going to hurt, right? I was still his friend, someone who cared greatly for him, just wasn't in love with him anymore. I placed a hand on his right shoulder. "Turn around and let's talk about this."

He spun around with tears in his eyes. I watched him toss the paper towels into the nearby wastebasket and he headed for the door. Over his left shoulder, he said, "You've made your point. There's nothing to talk about. Just as you said…it is what it is. We are over."

"Wait a minute." I sighed. "I don't want you to leave thinking I'm a villain. I just think it's a little selfish of you to think that your problems are my problems."

He shook his head. "You're not a villain. I would never think that way of you. Honestly, I respect and understand your position regarding Luanne. The woman is not your responsibility, and I get that. We're all old enough to take care of ourselves."

Our eyes connected for the briefest moment.

He said, "Look, I really have to go now."

I simply said, "Friends. We're still friends. As long as we're clear about that, okay?"

"Of course," he said, pulled the heavy door open, and left.

❖

Mother had fallen asleep in my office chair with her purse clutched in one hand and the empty bottle of gin in her other hand. What a pretty sight that was. One for the Christmas card. I removed the bottle from her grip, placed it on the edge of the desk, and decided to let her rest. Honestly, I wanted to call Victor Skoneski.

The alley had become my second office. Near the Dumpster I dialed Victor's number. A soft Russian voice said, "Hello, Victor Skoneski speaking."

"Victor, this is Troy Murdock. You don't know me but—"

"I do know you," Victor cut me off. "I have people watching you. I know too much about you and your life, if you want to know the truth."

How did he know me? Why did he have people watching me?

Victor said, "We meet in one hour."

"Why?"

"We meet at the Underground Man Club."

"Why?"

"I won't kill you. No. Have information for you." His responses floored me.

"Who are you and what is this all about, anyway?"

"One hour. This what I give you. If you don't show I understand you have no interest whatsoever to learn who try to murder Byron Copenrod."

"How do you know about that?"

Victor didn't answer my question. He had ended our call.

❖

"You're coming with me. I'm not about to do this alone and I need your help. Someone has to have my back," I demanded of Umberto.

Prissy Palentine had just driven away from the salon with an inebriated Mother at her side.

"Isn't your darling detective supposed to assist you in these matters? I thought he had your back, among other body parts."

"I can't reach him. He's at a meeting of some sort. That leaves you and me. Get ready to leave."

He spun around on his leather sandals and exclaimed, "Can't someone else help you? What about Ivan?"

"You're doing it!" I burst. "Something tells me this Victor guy is going to open the Pieney cases up for me by confessing important details he doesn't want anyone else to know."

"Why you? Shouldn't he just call the QV police? Do you really think this meeting with a complete stranger is safe?"

"I don't know," I replied. I didn't know.

"Don't tell me you're clairvoyant now."

"I never said that."

"Maybe you're not supposed to know these details concerning the killings, Troy."

"I'm not so sure about that. I just know that I have to check into this."

He sighed and rubbed the tip of his nose with two fingers. "Can I go like this?"

My friend was wearing a pair of men's white capris, Italian gold bracelets, and a tangerine blouse made of silk. I didn't want to offend him, but the Underground Man Club was not the place for his feminine blouse. Whips, leather, and chains were more acceptable. I knew he was sensitive about his outfits and stated in a rather polite manner, "That French leather number you own would be perfect for this occasion."

His eyes lighted with joy and a smirk of fascination covered his face. "The Marcus Trin jumpsuit? I've been dying to wear that!"

I directed him out of the salon and to my borrowed Buick. Once he was behind the wheel, ready to spin away from me, I said, "Do a quick change and meet me back here in thirty minutes. Victor will love the leather jumpsuit."

❖

The Underground Man Club was not exclusive. Umberto and I were familiar with the bar, having visited the racy club during our underage drinking years after high school. We had spent many evenings among the aggressive men, wide-eyed and nervous with our tongues out for various reasons. In fact, it was where I had met Ivan Reed years before on a glistening wet springtime night. The place was one story down, where badass leather types could find other men to play with.

The place smelled like smoke and cheap alcohol. The walls were painted coal-black and decorated with handcuffs, linked chains, and leather whips. Like any queer bar in Quill Village, the business was barely alive since it was still daylight. A few alcoholics, none of whom I knew, were seated around the oval bar. The drunks turned their blurred views to Umberto's all-black leather jumpsuit, which covered him from neck to ankles and enhanced all of his finely sculpted areas with visual delight.

One brawny drunk raised his beer and toasted Umberto. "Nice outfit! Come over here and do a dance for me, bitch!"

Umberto was flattered and would have gladly shared a dance with the burly dude had I not pushed him forward. Speedily, we passed the bar area and jukebox and headed into an unlit hallway marked *Daddy's Room*, which led to a back room where boys came out to play and became men, where leather-dressed businessmen enjoyed a spanking, and where handcuffs were just beginner toys for those interested in S&M.

Victor Skoneski exited Daddy's Room and stopped us. He was dressed in all black leather, just like Umberto. He had dark eyes, hair, and skin. I placed him in his mid-thirties, rigorous and damn sexy. We shared smiles as he checked out Umberto. "Nice suit. I see you came prepared for some excitement."

Umberto began to flirt. "The zipper goes from my neck to my cock. Do you want to try it out?"

"The zipper or your cock?" Victor asked in a sly and playful manner.

"The zipper, of course. It's shameful that I'm already taken."

Victor's dark eyes were magnetic. He said, "Too bad. We could get to know each other and have some fun fucking around, once you get out of that suit."

Before Umberto changed his mind about cheating on his Icelandic lover, I stepped around him and offered my hand for an introduction. "Troy...Troy Murdock."

Victor said, "I already know you. Now, let me guess, this delicious Cuban man is Umberto Clemente, your business partner. Is right?"

He did not shake my hand and I pulled it back. "Yes, you're correct."

Umberto asked with a sharp attitude, "How do you know so much about us?"

"Let's just say I have sources," Victor said.

"You a stalker?" Umberto questioned. "God knows I love a good stalker."

I lightly punched my cohort in his shoulder. "Stop it."

"I stalk when I have to," the bar owner said.

"Would you consider stalking me?"

"Why don't you come in office and I show you?" Victor suggested, and added, "I cause no problems for you. I only help."

He escorted us into his private office and served shots of Russian vodka over crushed ice; slivers of lime were added to the drinks. The office was decorated in bright reds and smelled of lavender. The Russian sat down behind his desk.

Umberto and I sat on the opposite side of the desk with our drinks.

I pulled out the list of ten names, placed it on Victor's glass desk, and pushed it to him. "Do you know these men?"

Victor nodded and said in his broken English, "The men and boys on list work for Blaine Phoenix."

Something in my gut had told me that. I asked, "You work for Phoenix, too, don't you?"

Victor nodded again. "Sometimes. It depends how busy with club, of course. We make fortune for Phoenix."

Umberto said, "You already make a fortune with this place. Why do you work for Phoenix?"

Victor shared his sexy smile again. He pointed at my friend and tol him, "The excitement. Why not? A man have his own fun, right?"

I added, "Until Ben Pieney got mixed into the lot. Do you want to help us understand that?"

Victor found a silver cigarette case on the surface of his desk and opened it. He offered Umberto and me cigarettes, but we declined. He removed one of the Camels for himself, but didn't light it. Instead, he toyed with it in his fingers. "Benny get greedy."

Umberto said, "He was wealthy. The league paid him millions. Why was he greedy?"

"Was it for control?" I asked. "Ben wasn't in it for the money, was he? Pieney wanted control."

Frustration surfaced on his face. He lit his cigarette.

"Start from the beginning. How did Ben Pieney get involved with Blaine Phoenix...and murder?"

Number nine on our list took another drag of his cigarette and blew a plume of blue-gray smoke into the room above our heads. He coughed, covered his mouth with a fist, and told us the story.

When Ben first got into Phoenix's private prostitution ring, it was all about the sex. Because the two were friends since childhood and trusted each other like blood brothers, Phoenix put Ben to work. Ben liked to experience different sexual adventures with an assortment of men. That lasted maybe the first eighteen months. He liked to have a lot of sex, which was making Phoenix very wealthy. Any questionable sexual pleasure you can possibly dream up: Sex with Daddies or older men. Sex with underage boys and go-go dancers. Ben was hired for private parties with no less than ten men at one shot. Trains ensued at a few of those parties. Weekend orgies were not uncommon. He was living for the sex, of course. And the more sex he had, the more money Phoenix raked in.

The problem started when Phoenix showed his pal how the business operated. The ins and outs and everything in detail. Ben learned quickly and studiously. He saw a great future for himself beyond the million-dollar throws. Phoenix had power over twenty or more guys, ten of whom were on his list. Ben wanted something more than a hometown quarterback's status, another reason why he was a big fan of the control factor. He wanted the power that Phoenix operated on, every ounce of it that he could obtain. He liked to be in charge on and off the field, and he didn't like that Phoenix called the shots in their shared game of prostitution. A power struggle ensued between the two men. Ben turned greedy and Phoenix turned angry, knowing the quarterback was attempting to take over his fortune. Ben wanted the sex, men, and money, whatever he could get his greedy hands on.

"And Phoenix murdered Pieney, getting rid of a problem. Right?" Umberto interrupted.

Our smoking suspect nodded and agreed. "He also nailed brother. Cort his name."

"Because Cort knew what Ben was doing outside of football," I said.

"Yes. The brothers very close. Phoenix had to off him."

"Jesus," Umberto said. "Their game was out of control."

Victor said, "Phoenix's game was murder."

"Why you?" I asked. "Why are you ratting out Blaine Phoenix?"

"I have reasons. Every man does." Victor was still.

"You're going to take over the boy business once Phoenix goes to jail, aren't you?" Umberto said.

Victor didn't respond. Language barrier or not, he knew our conversation had crossed many lines. Prostitution was illegal, which he also knew. Maybe the man had already said too much and realized it.

"Silence is the perfect answer," Umberto went on. "Of course you're taking over his fortune. A lot of money to be made. You'll be going from prostitute to pimp. The opportunity will be available once Phoenix is behind bars. The boy business legacy will thrive with you in charge. I'd probably take advantage of that prospect, too, if I ever had—"

"Let it go, Umberto," I warned. "I think we're done here. I'm sure Mr. Skoneski has a lot of work to do, and we're taking up too much of his time."

We stood and shook the man's hand over his glass desk.

"Thank you for seeing us," I said. "Ben would be proud of you for helping out."

"It was my pleasure," Victor replied.

CHAPTER EIGHTEEN
HIS SPELL

The landline phone in my apartment rang. I had accidentally turned my cell phone off and it was on its charger. It was Zane. "I need you, Troy."

"All the guys in the world need me. I should start charging every time I hear that. I'd be a millionaire by now and wouldn't have to operate Umberto's."

"Listen to me closely." His tone changed from upbeat to serious in a matter of seconds. "I want to talk to you about the Cutie Pie case. I believe we found our man. I think I know who murdered the Pieney brothers. Now we just have to land him."

"Who is it? Tell me now."

"I can't. Not over the phone. That's way too risky."

"You're being difficult, Zane. I have my own situation to handle." Wails ensued within my apartment: Ivan Reed was in the bathroom, sulking and broken.

"What kind of situation?"

"Ivan's here. He's sobbing all over the place and drowning in his own tears. Luanne dumped him with a Dear John letter and then she took off. I'm trying to be a good friend and take care of him. He's being a big baby, though, and I'm starting to lose my patience."

"Where is Luanne?"

"We don't know. She's been missing in action for the past twelve hours. Ivan's here for some support. He says he doesn't want to be alone. The poor bastard is so brokenhearted."

"Feed him some alcohol and drugs, and tell him to buck the fuck up. Then get your cute little ass over to my house for a Cutie Pie update. What I have to share with you is quite intriguing. Trust me, you won't be disappointed."

"I'll see what I can do, Zane. I can't promise anything, though."

"Of course you can. Ivan's a big boy. He can take care of himself."

"Let me wrap up things here and I'll be right over."

The little boy came out in him and he laughed. "Don't go. I know you miss me."

I did. More than he knew. I smiled. "I do miss you. Things are unequivocally boring without you around."

"What do you miss about me?"

"I can't believe the way you talk me into doing things. It's like I'm under a spell when I'm with you. I'm sure you've always wanted it that way."

"You have the wrong guy. I've never talked you into anything you didn't want to do."

"I have to go."

"Come visit me, Troy. The sooner the better."

"I will. As I already said, let me deal with Ivan and I'll be over."

"I'll wait up."

"I hope you do."

❖

Drugs and alcohol. I had Vicodin and beer, Valium and some Smirnoff, a drug called Entice and gin. No! Absolutely not! I wouldn't drug Ivan and leave. Instead, I placed a warm compress to his forehead and said, "The pain will go away with sleep."

Because I was a chivalrous ex-boyfriend, I gave up my bedroom to him. Ivan looked pitiable, pallid, and distressed. I listened to him mumble, "What have I done? Where has she fled? How can I go on from here?"

"You obviously love this woman, don't you?"

He shook his head. "I don't. Really. We just communicate well."

I wasn't about to argue with him. "Women are crazy. This is just one more reason why I like the company of men."

"I know she was the star actress performing in her dramas. I just can't imagine how a star could run away, though. The truth is biting. It's not fun to be unloved and disliked, as you probably already know."

"Don't forget that she's mentally unstable."

"I suppose." He nodded and wiped tears away from his eyes. Of course, he was being overdramatic just like Luanne. There was no point in arguing with him. Instead, I thought about the different drugs and alcohol throughout the apartment. I asked, "Would you like a pill with some vodka? Something to make this all better?"

He surprised me and nodded. "I would. It might work. Maybe I just need some sleep."

Before he changed his mind, I bolted away to the bathroom for two Valium, found the Smirnoff in the kitchen, and returned to his side.

"Three," he said. "I want three pills."

"Two will put you under a magical spell." I shook my head. "Three with alcohol is not a good idea."

"Two it is, then."

I passed the pills and glass of vodka to him. Ivan gulped the Smirnoff down like it was water. He wiped the back of his right hand across his mouth, sighed heavily, and passed the empty glass back to me.

He reached for my right hand with his left one and asked, "Can I tell you something?"

I nodded in agreement. Why not?

"You always know what to say to me when we're together. It's one of the things I like most about you."

"Thank you," I replied.

"I don't love her, Troy. I really want you to know that. I've always been in love with you."

Shit…what was going on? Obviously he'd had too much vodka; shame on me for feeding him drugs and alcohol.

Ivan squeezed my hand and said, "I regret our breakup. You were a good find and I blew it."

I nodded. "You're a very sweet man…one of the best, and look what I've done to us. I've created a catastrophe between us. I've broken a good thing."

The alcohol and pills spell were working their magic. His eyelids began to slip closed, slowly fluttered open, closed again, and he dramatically yawned. "I…I love you," were his last words before he passed out right before my eyes. He started to snore, caught up in numbed sleep, distance…lost and far away.

I escaped the apartment. What are friends for, right?

❖

"I can't talk right now, Mother."

"Are you on a date?"

"No. I'm solving a crime."

She laughed, which sounded a bit creepy. "You can be such a funny guy sometimes, Troy. Now, what are you really doing?"

"Driving to—"

Minnie cut off my explanation. "I'm calling your brother. I want to smooth out our differences. I've been completely unsupportive and rather mean to him lately."

"Who are you, and what have you done with Mother?" I asked in a playful manner.

"That's not funny, young man. Don't try to do your stand-up with me."

"I'm sorry," I said, and made a right onto Botcher Street. Zane's house was just a few more blocks away. "How did you come to this understanding?"

"My shrink said I can be cold and calculating at times. She never lies to me. After explaining my dislike for Beth Bradbaum, Dr. Wetzel suggested I should rethink my emotions toward the woman and begin to heal."

"Elizabeth," I corrected her.

"Yes, Elizabeth. It's going to take a while to get used to this. I just want you to know I'm working on it."

"I'm glad you're coming to your senses, Mother. To be frank with you, I was starting to think you were losing your mind."

Our connection became fuzzy and I lost her.

❖

7291 Zeus Drive. Zane's place was a contemporary designer's dream come true atop Quill Village's Mt. Sebastian: a robust dwelling with over six thousand square feet, willed to him by his wealthy uncle Carmichael following a mysterious shooting in Gladshire, Maine, two years before. The house was airy with large rooms, and of good taste. Zane had the place decorated by Alonzo Filigree, the same designer who'd added a burst of life to Umberto's pad. Rich reds, vibrant blues, and explosions of yellows filled the detective's abode.

He stood in front of a fully stocked bar and asked, "How would you like your martini this evening?"

"Make it dry with two olives."

"I aim to please."

We sat across from each other in stuffy, high-back reading chairs overlooking the southern side of Quill Village. I tried a sip of my martini and relished its smooth flavor. "I took your advice with Ivan and fed him some Valium and Smirnoff."

"And now he's sleeping like a baby, right?"

"Out like a light."

"Ahhh...the miracles one can perform with drugs and alcohol never cease to amaze me." Zane clinked his martini glass against mine. "To us and solving the Pieney case murders."

"Who is the killer? You tell me what you know and then I'll tell you what I know. What did you find out? I can barely wait another second."

He relaxed in his chair. Casually, he crossed one leg over the other and said, "Nina has the case solved. Her team should be arresting"—he looked down at his watch and examined the time—"Blaine Phoenix within the hour."

I told him about my findings with Umberto and our little escapade at the Underground Man Club.

He shared a smile with me and finished his drink.

"Tell me what you know about Phoenix. I'm all ears."

"Relax now and listen to everything I know."

"I can hardly wait. Do share."

He crossed his legs like a gentleman and began, "Phoenix knew Benjamin Pieney was going out on a date with you,

Troy. They've been friends for a lifetime, and saw each other three or four times a week. Phoenix set the first murder scene at your building while Pieney and you were messing around upstairs, inside your apartment. Phoenix placed a thin layer of tape over the door's lock, which allowed the door to close but prevented it from locking. The door looked and felt like it had locked, but it hadn't. Nina discovered the tape on the door once the Quill Village investigative team arrived at the scene on the morning of the murder. Phoenix's fingerprints were on the tape. Of course, we decided not to share that information with you. No offense."

"None taken," I replied.

"He kissed you good night and left. You went to bed. Phoenix, we have learned through a key witness, was seen outside Umberto's. The female witness, a tenant who lives in apartment 3-F across the street, stated that Phoenix attacked Pieney on the sidewalk. The barbed wire was used as well as the *Cutie Pie Must Die!* pin."

"Where did Phoenix get the barbed wire?" I asked.

"Ohio. We traced the wire to a Farm and Feed store outside of St. Clairsville. It's the only company that sells the stuff."

I asked, "What about the pins?"

"He got the pins from Trenton. They were specially made by a Chinese company called Tango's. He used the name P. Blane...B-l-a-n-e."

"So why did Phoenix kill Cort Pieney?"

"Because Cort knew too much about his brother's secret life."

"Secret life?" I questioned. "What do you mean by that?"

He raised his eyebrows and asked, "Any guesses?"

"Prostitution. The list we found inside Ben's aunt's bedroom organized Ben's clients."

"Wrong. They were his employees."

I shook my head, confused. "What do you mean?"

"On the night Ben was murdered, Phoenix said he was with a married woman by the name of Olivia Bain."

"I remember that. Did it check out?"

He shook his head, swallowed some of his fresh drink, and said, "I'm afraid not. With a little pressure, Olivia came clean and exposed Phoenix's prostitution ring. She wasn't with him on the night Ben was killed. She was with her husband in Boston. She confessed to me about Phoenix's ring."

"Ben was operating the ring? I thought Phoenix was."

Zane nodded and said, "You're very smart. Ben was trying to operate the business. The list of men we found in Ben's aunt's place was Phoenix's employees. Ben tried to take Phoenix's ring over and..."

"Ben was murdered because he was trying to take over the business."

"Right again, chap."

"And Cort knew what his brother was doing, which prompted Phoenix to off him." I paused, drank half of my martini. "Did Ben do it for the money?"

He abruptly shook his head. "Absolutely not. The football league paid him millions. He didn't need the money."

"Did he do it for the rush?"

"I think so. We'll never know the truth, though."

"He liked power and risk, on the field and off. It's too bad it got him killed."

"Some guys don't know when to stop, do they?" Zane sat his martini down on the walnut table between us, stood, and stepped up to me. He took my drink from my hands and placed it next to his. Before I knew it, he started to kiss me.

I pushed him away. "You should help Nina catch the bastard."

"I'm not on the clock. Besides, my job is done. The clues are collected and…"

"Does that matter, though?" I asked, unsure of his position's details. "You should help her."

"I only make the arrest when I clearly have to."

"Phoenix is dangerous. You should be out there helping Nina, no matter what."

"You don't understand. It would be crossing a line. I pulled the facts together and solved the crimes. Nina's job is to—"

I didn't want to hear it. "You end up putting those close to you in danger. You've done it to me and now you're doing it to Nina."

"That's not true."

I nodded, disappointed with him. "It is true. You almost killed me. Now Nina's in danger. You have no remorse about that, do you?"

"People have certain jobs. Nina's working with three other guys to take Phoenix down. I don't have to be there. I don't have to—"

Enough. I bolted from his house. Zane thought about himself a little too much at times. He didn't give a flying shit about what happened to the people around him. Putting lives in danger meant nothing to him. It seemed reckless and imprudent, something that I didn't find attractive in him.

❖

Less than thirty minutes later I was home again. I needed another drink to calm down, maybe even two sleeping pills like what I had given Ivan. I opened my front door and stepped inside quietly in hopes of not waking Ivan.

"Fuck!" I frantically flicked the living room's light switch up, down, up. The fuse had blown in the breaker box again—it happened regularly. The box was located in the laundry room, at the rear of the apartment, next to my bedroom. Carefully, I moved through the dark with outstretched arms. I banged into a wall, forehead and nose first. I saw brilliant yellow-gold stars.

The strange and aggressive voice was a deep whisper behind me: "Cutie pie must die."

I spun around but didn't see anyone. The darkness was coal black. Not even a shadow. Not a single movement. I swung my arms from left to right and felt nothing. I said, "Who's there?" but there was no reply. And then I felt a prick in my right biceps, deep and painful.

In a matter of seconds my legs buckled under my weight and I fell to the floor, closed my eyes, and drifted away in a deep sleep.

CHAPTER NINETEEN
YOU NAUGHTY MAN

When I came to, dizzy and dehydrated, I knew where Phoenix had taken me. In 2009 Quill Village High School was abandoned because of problems with asbestos. The edifice was to be torn down and the QV War Memorial Park was to be built. Political fighting had stopped the project and the high school was still standing. I hadn't been in the boys' locker room since I was in high school.

The air was stagnant in the abandoned locker room. My hands were tied behind my back with what felt like barbed wire. My ankles were also secured. I was seated in a student's metal chair with cotton shoved in my mouth, which was sealed with duct tape stuck to my cheeks.

I blinked a number of times. Directly in front of me were wooden benches positioned in front of the metal lockers. Showers were to the far left. A glassed-in coach's office was positioned at the locker room's rear.

Directly behind me, Phoenix whispered loudly, "I've underestimated you, Murdock. Your sleuthing has helped ruin me."

He stepped in front of me and began to pace. Phoenix was wearing a tight pair of running shorts and Nike shoes. His torso was chiseled in a white tee with a wide navy stripe running across his muscular chest. I saw a line of drying blood on his left forearm. While laboring over his third cigarette, filling the empty room with spirals of blue-gray smoke, he continued to pace. "Ben and I were lovers for a short period of time. I found it amazing to spend my life with him. The sex was great. I fell for him and, unfortunately, he broke my heart. Ben enjoyed a number of guys on the side. I could have handled his affairs. I understand a man's needs. His infidelity was not an issue for me. What I couldn't handle was his betrayal. Ben wanted more than boyfriends. He wanted my business. He wanted the power and control of a select group of hot men who could work for him. My hired help was soon going to be his hired help, if I didn't do something about it. He got greedy and wanted everything I had. I couldn't let that happen."

He shuffled a step closer to me. He ruffled my buzz cut with his right palm and whispered down at me, "Things are looking up, though. I can start over. There's a whole new world out there. I can create something twice the size this time around." After rubbing the top of my head, he pushed my head forward. "Guys like what I have to offer them, Mr. Murdock. They fall under my spell with ease, and I give them exactly what they want."

Phoenix pulled my head back by my hair. He quickly ripped the duct tape from my mouth and removed the cotton from inside.

I found the courage to say, "Please, don't hurt me. I'm an innocent party. You have to let me go. You have to understand that—"

He chortled. "It's not possible for me to be kind." He circled me again. "When you brought Detective Ward to my apartment to question me…"

He removed his right palm from my chin, smacked me on the back of the head with brutality, and…

Neither Ben nor Cort Pieney had been raped by Blaine

Phoenix. Yes, they were beaten. And yes, their windpipes had been sliced open with barbed wire. A vigorous chuckle surfaced from his lips and then he whispered, "I've changed my mind. I can't keep you. Although that was my first inclination after fetching you from your apartment tonight, I've decided you're a little too high maintenance for my needs. Truth is, Mr. Murdock, I don't have the patience for you. You scare me a little. And like the Pieney duo…Cutie Pie must die."

❖

I was hauled up and out of the chair, which he kicked away. The barbed wire was removed from my ankles and wrists. He slugged me in the face three more times, leaving me half-conscious. Phoenix found a pair of extra-thick black gloves, slipped them on, and placed a string of barbed wire around my neck, pulling on it with one fist, and started to choke me.

"On your hands and knees now! I'm going to fuck the nice boy out of you, Murdock. Do you understand me?"

I did.

"I'm going to make you bleed to death. And if I get bored with that…"

I was already bleeding from the mouth where he had bashed me with his fist numerous times. My temple bled and…

"Just so you know, buttercup, after I'm done fucking you, I'm going to murder you. You understand me, pal?" He pulled on the strand of barbed wire around my neck.

I felt two barbs enter my throat, which caused me to close my eyes and push the fresh pain away. I groaned in an animalistic way and he began to laugh.

If I was going to survive, I had to keep my strength. As Phoenix spanked my ass with his right palm, calling me the nastiest names, I began to plan my escape. My feet and ankles were not wrapped in barbed wire. The only problem I really faced was the barbed wire around my neck, which Phoenix held like a dog's leash. If I could just...

Fearing for my life, I felt the murderer's hands between my thighs. He spread my legs. "I just may fuck you after I kill you. Ain't nothing wrong with a cold lay, right?"

He pulled on the string of sharp barbed wire and the pointed metal dug deep into my neck, causing four nasty, deep gouges.

I heard the locker room's east door swing open on its rusty hinges, then the sound of heavy footsteps crossing the cement floor.

Phoenix said, "Who the fuck is that?"

Out of the corner of my right eye, I saw Phoenix reach down and to his left. He removed a Colt .45 off the floor, next to one of the benches.

The sounds of footsteps closed in on us. Detective Zane Ward appeared at the far end of the lockers. In his right hand, he held a 9mm, which he cocked and aimed at my abductor. Zane said, "Let him go, Phoenix. He's not who you want and you know it."

Phoenix popped off a shot at Zane. The loud bang echoed off the tiled walls and the bullet from his .45 smashed three tiles just above the cop's head.

I made eye contact with Zane. My head stung with fresh pain and my neck hurt from the barbed wire. My entire body was tense and stiff. I couldn't even move a muscle.

Zane held his 9mm in front of him and pulled the trigger.

The bullet slammed into my right shoulder. I felt a warm stinging sensation mixed with punctured flesh. More pain arced through my upper body. I began to shiver on the cement floor and floated into semiconsciousness. Blood began to cover my chest. I tried to make eye contact with Zane, but my lids closed…opened…closed…and opened.

More bullets. Again, I screamed. It sounded like a war zone inside the locker room. Bullets exploded tile, which shattered and dropped all around me.

Phoenix took a slug in his gut that knocked him backward and to the cement floor. The Colt dropped to the floor. Phoenix let out a thunderous roar and banged his head on the cement beneath him.

Zane rushed to my side, falling to his knees. Panicked, tears springing to life in his eyes, he ran his right palm over my head and said, "Jesus, Troy, I didn't mean it."

"You shot me," I gurgled.

Zane wrapped his shirt around his hands and untwisted the barbed wire from around my neck, careful not to rip either of us to shreds. He promised, "It's going to be all right. I'm going to get you out of here and to a hospital. I can make this better."

"Shot…me," I mumbled. "Tried…kill me."

He kissed my forehead and stood with me in his hulking arms, sending another bolt of severe pain through my right shoulder. "I'm taking you to my cruiser. I'm driving you to the hospital myself. No need to worry. You're in good hands."

Once in his cruiser, Zane used his cell phone and rattled off instructions. "I'm leaving now for the hospital. Troy is losing a lot of blood."

Prior to passing out, I heard him say something soft and sweet: "I got you, babe. You're not going to die on my shift. I love you too much for that to happen."

CHAPTER TWENTY
UNDER THE BLUE GRILL'S CANOPY

R oom 722 in QV Hospital had mint-green walls, ivory-colored blinds, and a black-and-white checkered floor. I felt safe there, in good hands.

Approximately twenty hours after the slug was removed from my right shoulder, Ivan Reed visited me with a handful of flowers and chocolates. He placed the flowers next to my window, which overlooked Lake Quill, and found a seat next to my bed in an uncomfortable-looking chair. He leaned forward and kissed my forehead. He said with a smile, "You are loved."

"I'm in pain. My shoulder is killing me and the codeine pills aren't working as well as I'd like."

"You're a lucky bastard. Phoenix almost killed you. Your face is all over the news, on every channel. People are saying what a brave man you are."

I said, "It's bullshit. I was just trying to protect Zane like—"

"Enough," Ivan said and pressed two fingers against my mouth. "You're getting worked up over nothing. I came to share other news with you, of course."

I pushed his fingers away. "What kind of news?"

"I met a new woman. Her name is Sylvia Marigold and she's blind. She's a member of the QV Blind Association.

I want to help her out for two hours a day, hopefully in the evenings. We'll see what happens."

I asked, "You like helping women, don't you?"

"Everyone has a gift."

"Tell me a little about Sylvia. Where does she live? Who does she hang with? What does she see in a nice schmuck like you?"

"She's a painter who lives at Anders Hall. She has this amazing brother who just happens to be gay and…"

"He likes you, doesn't he?"

He nodded. "And I like him."

"What is this guy's name?"

"Andy Marigold." Ivan shook his head. "He's very butch. A man's kind of man. All muscle and roughness. Andy likes boots and jeans and big belt buckles. He enjoys country music and beer."

I was happy for him.

About twenty minutes after Ivan left, Nina Bowel came into my room. She crossed her hands at her waist and said, "I have a serious question for you, Murdock." Her thin eyebrows slanted and her neck cords tightened.

"What is it?"

"It's personal."

"Ask away, Nina. God knows I'm not going anywhere but this bed."

"How do you feel about Detective Ward?"

"I like him. He's a nice guy."

"How much do you like him?"

"Look, Nina, cut to the chase already. What's your point? Why are you really here?"

"Zane and I not only are partners, but we're also close friends. The only thing he seems to be talking about lately is you. The guy thinks you're a million bucks, Troy."

"That's a lot of feeling."

"This is why I'm here. I'm more concerned about Zane than you."

"Are you attempting to hook us up as a permanent couple with each other?"

"Whatever it takes. I'm his partner. We look out for each other. It's my duty to help him."

"And Zane's happy with me?" I asked.

"About as happy as he can get."

❖

Cody couldn't make it to the hospital, but he did call. He shared the most exciting news with me: "I've asked Liz to marry me. We're thinking of a December wedding next year."

"That's wonderful!" I beamed. "My older brother is finally getting hitched."

"You can't tell a soul yet. If Mother catches wind of this, she'll have to be committed to the Fern Hill Home for the next year."

"My lips are sealed."

"You can't tell Umberto, either. Promise me you won't. That man's lips flap a little too much."

"I promise not to tell Umberto."

"Mother cannot, I repeat, cannot find out about this."

"She won't from me. I promise." I meant that. Unlike Umberto, I was pretty reliable about keeping secrets.

He filled me in on the preliminary plans for their extraordinary day. Liz wanted a small ceremony on a snowy day in Rossmore Park. There would be no bridesmaids or groomsmen, no screaming children, and—if Liz had her way—Mother would be drunk, since that was when she was most kind.

"It sounds delightful, Cody. I'm so happy for you. Congratulations. She's going to make a wonderful sister-in-law, and a lovely wife to you."

"According to Mother, as soon as you get out of that hospital we are having another family dinner. I plan on breaking the news to her about marrying Liz."

"I'll say a little prayer for the two of you to get through this."

"Thank you, little brother. That means the world to me. You're so good to me."

❖

Umberto and Axel arrived two days after Cody's call and rescued me from QV Hospital. They drove me back to my apartment, chatting about absolutely nothing important the entire way.

I learned that the staff was running the salon. Umberto decided to stay upstairs to take care of me, making sure I was comfortable, had enough food in the apartment to survive, and had plenty of magazines to thumb through.

"I'll be your nurse for the next three days. When I'm not around, Axel will be taking care of you." He opened a window.

"You're spoiling me. I think I can make it on my own."

He shook his head. "I don't think so. We have to get you to one hundred percent in less than a week."

I stared at him and said, "Something's going on that you're not telling me."

"I can never hide a secret, can I? Shame on me. I'm half-embarrassed."

"Don't be, biscuit. Now, spill the beans."

He stood at the foot of my bed. "I'll give you three guesses. Begin."

"You're going on vacation outside of the country."

He clapped his hands with excitement. "How'd you know?"

"It was a lucky guess. Where are you going, and with whom?"

"Axel invited me to Buenos Aires for two weeks. Will you watch the store until I return?"

"Of course!"

For the next half hour he sat at my right side and filled me in on all the details. "Now for the serious stuff."

"What serious stuff?"

"Detective Zane Ward stuff."

"Shit. I thought he was out of my life." I rolled my eyes.

"Why would you want to dispose of him?"

"Dispose sounds like murder. I just want some space from him."

"Do you know that he called me?"

I shook my head. "He didn't. You're lying. Why would he call you?"

"Why would I lie about that? He spilled his guts about you. Troy this and Troy that stuff. I think you're being a little hard-assed about seeing him. Give the guy a chance. I'm talking about a few dates. The guy really likes you and you ignore him. The Pieney murders are solved, and…you ditched the guy."

"He tries to kill me every time we're together."

"Give him a break."

"I'll think about it," I said, "but I can't promise anything."

He stood over me, wagging a finger. "He's not asking for

a long-term relationship or marriage, Troy. He's not asking for monogamy or every holiday spent together for the next six years. The guy simply wants a date with you. I think you're losing out. Maybe you should think about changing your attitude and lighten up a bit. Zane's a nice guy. You're a nice guy. I see chemistry there. If you're going to think about it, think hard, and fast. He might just get away from you and it will be too late."

"I will," I said.

"I mean it, Troy. Zane's a nice guy. And both of us know that nice guys are very hard to come by."

"I understand, Umberto, honestly."

He moved up to the bed again and kissed my forehead. "I'm looking out for your best interest, pal…that's all I'm doing."

"I know. Thank you."

"You'll thank me later, I'm sure. For now, just think it through."

❖

Chasing a guy was not my forté. Zane was special, though, wasn't he? I had yearned to see his sexy body again. I wanted to hold him against my skin and have him kiss the length of my neck, and…whatever else a hot detective's mouth could do. Seeing him was out of the question, though. Zane and I were trouble together. He was exactly what I wanted, and exactly what I didn't want.

Besides, if he really liked me, why wasn't he chasing me?

❖

Mother decided to have a welcome-home dinner party for me.

Soon after my arrival, Liz prepared blue martinis and passed them around with a glowing smile. Mother seemed relaxed in Liz's company, consuming one drink after another without watching her intake. She grew giddy and wide-eyed as she served cheese puff appetizers with morsels of bacon and pineapple.

We all stood in a semicircle in the dining room next to the table. Cody sat on the window seat overlooking the driveway. He asked, "Troy, is your lover boy coming this evening?"

"I don't have a lover boy." I took a sip of my fresh drink.

Mother waved a hand at me. "That Zane Ward is who you should be with. I adore him. He's an angel sent from heaven."

I said, "I'm perfectly healthy as a single, people."

My shoulder still hurt. It was healing slowly. A scar would always remind me of the Piney brothers and my short adventure with Zane.

"That's too bad, Troy. Zane is such a nice young man. Quite the looker, if you ask me. I would really like to see my baby become serious with him." Obviously the alcohol was talking rather than the woman who birthed me.

Liz added her two cents. "You two have chemistry. You click. The room lights up when you're together."

"Zane is far too dangerous for me."

Cody said, "There's nothing safe about you, little brother, and there never has been. Why are you so worried about Zane hurting you?"

A timer went off in the kitchen, prompting a break in the conversation. Mother vanished into the kitchen, and Liz refilled our drinks. I sat down at the table across from Cody.

I asked, "Are you breaking the news tonight to Mother about marrying Liz?"

Cody nodded, nervously smiling. "I plan on feeding her another drink before that happens."

"Two drinks."

"Three," Liz said from behind me, "just to be safe."

Mother served mostly finger foods, since my right arm was still in a sling. Dinner was garlic-provolone chicken fingers, asparagus spears in lemon butter, and seasoned potato bites fried crispy in a light olive oil.

Liz and Cody sat on one side of the square table and Mother sat next to me on the opposite side. We were not more than ten minutes into the meal when Mother spotted the rock on Liz's finger.

"Beth, what's that on your finger?"

Cody stepped up to bat. "Liz and I are engaged, Mother. I want her to be my wife."

Mother lost most of the color in her face. She reached across the table and took Liz's left hand. "You are so coy, Cody...just like your father!" She smiled. "Shame on you for not telling me about this wonderful news before!"

I let out a deep sigh of relief.

Liz sighed with gratitude.

Cody looked confused.

Mother jumped up from her chair and skirted around the table. She flung herself against the thin and frail woman with the diamond ring. Mother wrapped her arms around her future daughter-in-law's neck and yelled, "My son is getting married! I never thought this day would happen! I'm going to have grandbabies!"

Cody had tears in his eyes. Before I knew it, we were all standing, sharing a group hug, laughing and celebrating the exciting news.

❖

I decided not to go home after dinner at Mother's because I drank too much and was missing Zane Ward. I was feeling a bit blue. The Diva Club on Edwardian Avenue called to me, and I needed a strong nightcap.

It was early in the evening and pouring down rain outside. The club had about ten people inside. Smitty, the club's twenty-nine-year-old co-owner, served me my desired and needed Long Island iced tea. He placed the drink in front of me on a dainty napkin and said, "Enjoy."

On the opposite side of the dark and smoke-filled bar, I watched Kenny Manderon, a Diva regular and Smitty's current flame, pop quarters into the jukebox. About seven seconds later one of my favorite songs of all time filled the Diva Club: Lady Gaga's "You and I."

How long was I sitting there? An hour? Two hours? I drank three Long Islands, listened to a variety of disco songs, and watched Smitty serve his boyfriend kisses and strong drinks.

I felt a palm on my good shoulder. Someone behind me breathed on the back of my neck. Before I could turn around, Zane whispered into my right ear, "I've missed you, Troy. I've been going crazy without you."

I turned and looked over my shoulder. There he was, the man who shot me. I said, "I'm still mad at you. If I didn't know you, my injury would have never happened."

Zane sat in the chair next to me. He placed his left palm on my right thigh and said, "Is this why you're avoiding me?"

"I'm not avoiding you. I'm merely recovering."

"From us or your wound?"

"Both, Zane."

"I visited you at the hospital three times. You were

sleeping. I took you flowers, a stuffed bear, two books to read, and a basket of fruit."

"I got them."

"I said I was sorry," he said.

"I know." My heart was racing and my mind started to spin. Maybe I had too many songs and Long Islands. Maybe I was in lust. Or maybe I was no longer angry at him. I found two twenties from my wallet and placed them on the bar, jumped off the stool, and walked out.

He followed me out of the club. At the top of the stairs he pulled me under the Blue Grill's canopy and pressed the back of my arms against the red brick wall. As thunder rumbled and lightning raced across the July sky, he positioned his face against mine. He growled, "I'm not perfect, Troy. No guy is. We all make mistakes in life. Many accidents happen, but..."

I felt his breath against my lips. Our chests touched. I said, "What?"

"Do you think I'm sexy?"

"You're not, Zane," I lied.

"You want to kiss me."

"I don't." I shook my head.

"And you missed me. I know you have...just as much as I missed you."

"Never," I whispered, feeling his breath against my breath, suffering from a spell of light-headedness...lust...something.

"You need me in your life, Troy Murdock. We're a great team together. It's time you admit that to yourself, and to me."

I felt on fire against the brick wall, sick to my stomach, dizzy and confused. I needed another Long Island. I needed...

He said, "You like the danger. You were getting off on it, just like you get off on me. I'm you're Mr. Right and you know it, Troy."

I was speechless, intoxicated by him, in lust, or love, or something that I knew was going to last a long time.

"I caught you," he said. "And I don't intend to let you go."

"You're dangerous," I whispered, wanting to kiss him.

"I'm not going anywhere."

Before I could reply, he leaned into me and kissed me.

About the Author

R. W. Clinger is a resident of Pittsburgh. He has a degree in English from Point Park University of Pittsburgh. His writing entails gay human studies. His work includes the novels *Just a Boy*, *Skin Tour*, *Skin Artist*, *Soft on the Eyes*, *Pool Boy*, and *The Last Pile of Leaves*. Rob has published many stories with StarBooks Press as well as *The Weekender*, a novella with Dreamspinner Press. *The Boyfriend Season and Other Stories*, his first book of shorts, is published with JMS Books, as well as the novellas *The Author's Assistant*, *Torso Tackle*, *Front Loader*, *Beneath his Stolen Skin*, *Beneath the Boarder*, and *Nebraska Close*. His novellas include *Frat Brats*, *Panama Dan*, *Spoil Me So*, *The Shower Police*, and *Splash Boys*. He continues to add to his Stockton County Cowboys Series, which includes *Chasing Cowboys*, *Riding Cowboys*, and *Roping Cowboys*. R. W. is currently at work on a second Troy Murdock and Zane Ward mystery.

Books Available From Bold Strokes Books

The Seventh Pleiade by Andrew J. Peters. When Atlantis is besieged by violent storms, tremors, and a barbarian army, it will be up to a young gay prince to find a way for the kingdom's survival. (978-1-60282-960-2)

Cutie Pie Must Die by R.W. Clinger. Sexy detectives, a muscled quarterback, and the queerest murders...when murder is most cute. (978-1-60282-961-9)

Going Down for the Count by Cage Thunder. Desperately needing money, Gary Harper answers an ad that leads him into the underground world of gay professional wrestling—which leads him on a journey of self-discovery and romance. (978-1-60282-962-6)

Light by 'Nathan Burgoine. Openly gay (and secretly psychokinetic) Kieran Quinn is forced into action when self-styled prophet Wyatt Jackson arrives during Pride Week and things take a violent turn. (978-1-60282-953-4)

Baton Rouge Bingo by Greg Herren. The murder of an animal rights activist involves Scotty and the boys in a decades-old mystery revolving around Huey Long's murder and a missing fortune. (978-1-60282-954-1)

Anything for a Dollar, edited by Todd Gregory. Bodies for hire, bodies for sale—enter the steaming hot world of men who make a living from their bodies—whether they star in porn, model, strip, or hustle—or all of the above. (978-1-60282-955-8)

Mind Fields by Dylan Madrid. When college student Adam Parsh accepts a tutoring position, he finds himself the object of the dangerous desires of one of the most powerful men in the world—his married employer. (978-1-60282-945-9)

Greg Honey by Russ Gregory. Detective Greg Honey is steering his way through new love, business failure, and bruises when all his cases indicate trouble brewing for his wealthy family. (978-1-60282-946-6)

Lake Thirteen by Greg Herren. A visit to an old cemetery seems like fun to a group of five teenagers, who soon learn that sometimes it's best to leave old ghosts alone. (978-1-60282-894-0)

Deadly Cult by Joel Gomez-Dossi. One nation under MY God, or you die. (978-1-60282-895-7)

The Case of the Rising Star: A Derrick Steele Mystery by Zavo. Derrick Steele's next case involves blackmail, revenge, and a new romance as Derrick races to save a young movie star from a dangerous killer. Meanwhile, will a new threat from within destroy him, along with the entire Steele family? (978-1-60282-888-9)

Big Bad Wolf by Logan Zachary. After a wolf attack, Paavo Wolfe begins to suspect one of the victims is turning into a werewolf. Things become hairy as his ex-partner helps him find the killer. Can Paavo solve the mystery before he runs into the Big Bad Wolf? (978-1-60282-890-2)

The Plain of Bitter Honey by Alan Chin. Trapped within the bleak prospect of a society in chaos, twin brothers Aaron and Hayden Swann discover inner strength in the face of tragedy and search for atonement after betraying the one you most love. (978-1-60282-883-4)

The Moon's Deep Circle by David Holly. Tip Trencher wants to find out what happened to his long-lost brothers, but what he finds is a sizzling circle of gay sex and pagan ritual. (978-1-60282-870-4)

Tricks of the Trade: Magical Gay Erotica, edited by Jerry L. Wheeler. Today's hottest erotica writers take you inside the sultry, seductive world of magicians and their tricks—professional and otherwise. (978-1-60282-781-3)

Straight Boy Roommate by Kevin Troughton. Tom isn't expecting much from his first term at University, but a chance encounter with straight boy Dan catapults him into an extraordinary, wild weekend of sex and self-discovery, which turns his life upside down, and leads him into his first love affair. (978-1-60282-782-0)

In His Secret Life by Mel Bossa. The only man Allan wants is the one he can't have. (978-1-60282-875-9)

Promises in Every Star, edited by Todd Gregory. Acclaimed gay erotica author Todd Gregory's definitive collection of short stories, including both classic and new works. (978-1-60282-787-5)

Raising Hell: Demonic Gay Erotica, edited by Todd Gregory. Hot stories of gay erotica featuring demons. (978-1-60282-768-4)

Pursued by Joel Gomez-Dossi. Openly gay college student Jamie Bradford becomes romantically involved with two men at the same time, and his hell begins when one of his boyfriends becomes intent on killing him. (978-1-60282-769-1)

Timothy by Greg Herren. *Timothy* is a romantic suspense thriller from award-winning mystery writer Greg Herren set in the fabulous Hamptons. (978-1-60282-760-8)

In Stone by Jeremy Jordan King. A young New Yorker is rescued from a hate crime by a mysterious someone who turns out to be more of a something. (978-1-60282-761-5)

Combustion by Daniel W. Kelly. Bearish detective Deck Waxer comes to the city of Kremfort Cove to investigate why the hottest men in town are bursting into flames in broad daylight. (978-1-60282-763-9)

Strange Bedfellows by Rob Byrnes. Partners in life and crime, Grant Lambert and Chase LaMarca are hired to make a politician's compromising photo disappear, but what should be an easy job quickly spins out of control. (978-1-60282-746-2)

The Jesus Injection by Eric Andrews-Katz. Murderous statues, demented drag queens, political bombings, ex-gay ministries, espionage, and romance are all in a day's work for a top secret agent. But the gloves are off when Agent Buck 98 comes up against the Jesus Injection. (978-1-60282-762-2)

Night Shadows: Queer Horror edited by Greg Herren and J.M. Redmann. *Night Shadows* features delightfully wicked stories by some of the biggest names in queer publishing. (978-1-60282-751-6)

Secret Societies by William Holden. An outcast hustler, his unlikely "mother," his faithless lovers, and his religious persecutors—all in 1726. (978-1-60282-752-3)

The Jetsetters by David-Matthew Barnes. As rock band the Jetsetters skyrocket from obscurity to superstardom, Justin Holt, a lonely barista, and Diego Delgado, the band's guitarist, fight with everything they have to stay together, despite the chaos and fame. (978-1-60282-745-5)

The Dirty Diner: Gay Erotica on the Menu, edited by Jerry L. Wheeler. Gay erotica set in restaurants, featuring food, sex, and men—could you really ask for anything more? (978-1-60282-677-9)

Sweat: Gay Jock Erotica by Todd Gregory. Sizzling tales of smoking-hot sex with the athletic studs everyone fantasizes about. (978-1-60282-669-4)

The Marrying Kind by Ken O'Neill. Just when successful wedding planner Adam More decides to protest inequality by quitting the business and boycotting marriage entirely, his only sibling announces her engagement. (978-1-60282-670-0)